DINOSAUR CANYON

Another 'You Say Which Way' Adventure
by
Blair Polly

Published by:
The Fairytale Factory Ltd.
Wellington, New Zealand.
All rights reserved.
Copyright Blair Polly © 2015

ISBN-13: 978-1519732699
ISBN-10: 1519732694

How This Book Works

- This story depends on YOU.

- YOU say which way the story goes.

- What will YOU do?

At the end of each chapter, you get to make a decision. Turn to the page that matches your choice. For example, **P62** means turn to page 62.

On a field trip to Montana, you see a meteorite streak across the sky. Heading out to find it starts a chain of adventures, including a trip back in time. Will you tell your teacher where you've been? Will you take him back to prove it? This 'You Say Which Way' book is packed with prehistoric possibilities!

Oh … and watch out for the T. Rex, he's hungry!

Dinosaur Canyon

At the campsite.

A meteorite streaks across a cloudless Montana sky and disappears behind a hill, not far away.

"Anyone see that?" you say to your classmates as you point towards the horizon.

Around the bus, a couple of students look up from their phones. "What? Huh?"

"The meteorite. Did you see it?"

"Meteor what?" the kid sitting next to you asks.

"Never mind." You shake your head and wonder if you're the only one who's really interested in this fieldtrip.

"I saw it," Paulie Smith says from a seat near the back. "That was amazing!"

As you and Paulie search the sky for more meteorites, the bus turns off the main road and passes an old wooden sign.

WELCOME TO GABRIEL'S GULCH.

"Right," Mister Jackson says, as the bus comes to a stop. "Once your tents are set up, you've got the afternoon to go exploring. So get to it. And remember, take notes on what you see and hear. You *will* be tested."

You're hoping to find some fossils. You might even get lucky and stumble across a piece of that meteorite. That would be awesome.

After locating a level patch of ground near a clump of saltbush, you set up your dome tent and toss your sleeping bag and air mattress inside with the rest of your gear. Then you grab your daypack and water bottle. You'd never think of going for a hike without taking water with you. They don't call this area the *Badlands* without good reason.

A couple of energy bars, an apple, compass, box of matches, waterproof flashlight, folding army shovel and some warm clothing go into your daypack as well, just in case.

Mister Jackson is drinking coffee with some parents who've come along to help. They've set up the kitchen near the junction of a couple of old stone walls as protection from the wind and are laughing and telling tales of other camping trips.

"My tent's up Mister J, so I'm off to look around."

He nods. "Make sure you fill in the logbook with your intentions. Oh, and who're you teaming up with? Remember our talk on safety – you're not allowed to go wandering about alone. And watch out for rattlesnakes."

You look at the chaos around camp. Rather than being interested in dinosaur fossils, which is the main reason for this trip, most of your fellow students are puzzling over how their borrowed tents work or complaining about the cell phone reception. Camping equipment is strewn everywhere. Apart from you, Paulie is the only one who's managed to get his tent up so far.

"Hey, Paulie. I'm heading out. Want to tag along?"

Paulie points to his chest. "Who? Me?"

Paulie's not really a friend. He's a year behind you at school, but at least he seems interested in being here. He's even got a flag with a picture of a T. Rex working at the front counter of a burger joint, flying over his tent. Chuckling, you ponder the silliness of a short-armed dinosaur flipping burgers

"Yeah, you, get a move on." You walk over and write in the camp's log book. *Going west towards hills with Paulie. Back in time for dinner.*

"What are we going to do?" Paulie asks.

"Explore those hills," you say, pointing off into the west. "Quick, grab your pack and let's go … before Mr. J or one of the parents decide to come along."

As Paulie shoves a few supplies in his bag, you look across the scrubland towards the badly-eroded hills in the distance. It's ideal country for finding fossils. Erosion is the fossil hunter's best friend. Who knows what the recent rains have uncovered for a sharp-eyed collector like yourself.

"Did you know they've found Tyrannosaurus Rex bones around here?" Paulie says as the two of you head out of camp.

You pull the *Pocket Guide to the Montana Badlands* out of your back pocket and hold it up. "I've been reading up too."

"But did you know scientists reckon T. Rex had arms about the same length as man's but would have been strong enough to bench press over 400 pounds?"

"Yeah?" you say, remembering Paulie's love of obscure facts and how he drives everyone at school crazy with them. "Well according to this book, there's been more dinosaur fossils found in Montana than anywhere else in the country."

Paulie nods. "I want to find an Ankylosaurus. They're built like a tank with armor and everything. They had horns sticking out of the sides of their heads and a mean looking club on the end of their tails!"

That would be pretty awesome. "A tank eh? Maybe we'll find one of its scales embedded in the rock, or a horn sticking out of a cliff. Anything's possible when fossil hunting, that's what makes it so exciting."

You both stride off across the prairie with big smiles and high hopes. Fifteen minutes later, when you look back, the camp is nothing but a cluster of dots barely visible through the sagebrush.

"Where to from here?" Paulie asks.

"There's a couple of options. We could search for that meteorite. It must have come down somewhere around here."

"Maybe it landed in that canyon?" Paulie says, indicating a gap between two hills. "Could be all sorts of neat stuff in there."

"That's Gabriel's Gulch," you say, referring to the map in

your guide. "Or we could look for fossils in those hills," you say, pointing to your right. "According to the guide, there's an abandoned mine over there too."

Your adventure is about to begin. It is time to make your first decision. Do you:

Go left into Gabriel's Gulch? **P6**

Or

Go right towards the eroded hills? **P11**

6

You have decided to go left into Gabriel's Gulch.

The canyon is narrow with a dried creek bed running down its centre. Wind and rain have sculpted the sandstone cliffs on either side into unusual shapes. You've followed the creek up for about a mile when you see a graceful sandstone arch sitting on a narrow ridge high above the canyon's floor.

"Wow," Paulie says. "Look at that." He pulls out his cell phone to take a picture.

"Let's climb up and get a closer look," you say. "We can take some shots of us standing beside it."

Paulie likes your idea and hurries along the gully spouting facts as he goes. "Did you know sandstone dates back to the Late Cretaceous period?"

You shake your head. "Do you live on Google, Paulie?"

"But–but that was the time of the dinosaurs. Everyone knows that!"

You're not sure that everyone does, but you do remember reading something in your guide book about this place. "It says here that Gabriel's Arch was named after the man who discovered it in 1802. It also says he died after being bitten by a rattlesnake a week later."

"Don't rattlesnakes rattle if you get near them?" Paulie asks.

"Unless you sneak up on 'em," you say. "Then they strike first and rattle later."

"Oh no!" Paulie says in mock terror, flapping his hands in exaggerated fashion and whipping his head back and forth faster than spectators at a tennis match.

"Don't give yourself whiplash," you say, trying not to crack up at his antics.

Paulie giggles. "I'm not afraid of snakes. Snakes are awesome. Our friends even. They get rid of the vermin. Besides, they're more afraid of you than you are of them."

He stops playing around and leads you up a washed out section of canyon wall and then up along a narrow ridge. Near the end of the ridge, a stone arch soars above you like a gateway to some mythical kingdom. Beyond the arch, the ridge comes to an abrupt end and a vertical cliff drops to the canyon floor. Across the canyon, in the distance, layered hills rise from a barren landscape to a clear blue sky.

As you walk towards the arch, you spot a fist-sized piece of rock that looks strangely out of place here in the Badlands. Rather than being ochre or tan – the colors usually associated with this part of the country – this rock is dark charcoal and covered in glassy specks and tiny holes. You wonder if it's volcanic in origin, but when you pick it up and feel its weight, you instantly know what you've found.

"Paulie, look. This could be that meteorite we saw."

Paulie looks down at the piece of rock in your hand. "How do you know?"

"See this blackish crust? This side would have taken all the heat as the rock burned its way through the atmosphere."

Paulie touches the pitted surface with his finger.

"And feel how heavy it is. Iron most likely."

Paulie tests the weight in his palm. "Wow, it is heavy!"

You can't wait to show this to Mister Jackson. With the hunk of rock in your hand, you walk towards the sandstone arch. "Take a photo of me in the arch with it, Paulie."

"I'll set the timer and get us both in the picture," Paulie says, placing the phone on a nearby boulder and adjusting its angle. "Right, get into position, we've got 10 seconds."

As you wait under the arch, the rock in your hand glows red and starts to vibrate, slowly at first, then faster and faster. A high-pitched hum gets louder and louder. You drop the lump and place your hands over your ears.

Paulie's eyes are scrunched closed and his hands are over his ears too. "Owwwwww!" he yells.

Then, with a bright flash, the sound stops.

Paulie looks at you in confusion. "Holy moly, what the heck was that?"

"I don't know, but it was awfully strange. Rocks don't normally make a–" And then you notice the landscape around you has changed.

What was semi-desert is now lush and green with broad-leafed plants and ferns. The dry grasslands have turned into a steamy jungle.

Paulie's notices it too and stands there wide-eyed and trembling. "Wha–what's going on? Am I dreaming?"

"This is impossible," you say, looking through the arch into the canyon. "Where did all this water come from?" Blinking, you try to make the illusion go away. "I don't think you're dreaming, Paulie." You pinch your forearm. "Ouch! I'm not."

"It's a lot warmer too," Paulie says. "And humid, like in the tropics."

Along the ridge, ferns and other tropical plants crowd a narrow, muddy path. The soles of your boots sinks into the soft soil, leaving footprints as you walk down it.

"Wait for me," Paulie yells, scurrying after you.

"I see animal prints," you say.

Paulie looks down and sees the impressions left by your boots. "So do I. What happened to the heel of your boot, it looks all chewed up?"

"My dog took a bite out of it," you say as you crouch down. "The boots still work okay though. But that's not the prints I'm talking about."

You point at the strange shapes in the mud. It's like a huge chicken has just walked by. "This must be an ostrich, or maybe an emu."

Paulie's eyes are wide. "I don't th–think so. It's way too big for that."

Your speculation is cut short when a strange lizard, about six-feet-long and three-feet-tall, scuttles into view from further down the ridge.

The creature looks at you, flicks its tongue a couple times, hisses, then stretches its long neck in your direction. It hisses again, snaps its teeth and moves towards you. It does not look friendly.

"Paulie, run!"

It is time to make a very quick decision. Do you:

Run back and climb the arch. **P15**

Or

Head back down into the canyon. **P20**

You have decided to go right, towards the eroded hills.

"Those hills look perfect for fossils," you tell Paulie. "Some may have washed out in the last rains."

"Now we just have to find them," Paulie says as the two of you veer right and pick up your pace.

As you walk, you scan the ground for rattlesnakes, just in case. Although rattlesnakes usually rattle when they sense a person coming, it never hurts to take a few extra precautions this far from medical help.

"Look there, Paulie," you say, pointing at a long S-shaped groove in the sandy ground. "That's a snake track if ever I saw one."

Paulie squats down and runs a finger along the groove. "Did you know there are 30 different species of rattlesnake in the world?"

"Really? That many?"

"But only one lives in Montana," he says with a smile. "So don't worry."

As you get closer to the hills, the layers of rock become more distinct. Like a cake with hundreds of thin layers ranging in color from light grey, to beige, tan, brown and even orange and pale yellow, they rise from the flatland around them. Some layers show the volcanic origins of this area, while others are fossilized sediments, laid down when the area was covered in a vast inland sea millions of years ago. Along with these sediments, the bones of many dinosaurs have been found.

After reaching the base of the hills, you stop briefly and refer to your guide. "There's meant to be a trail around here somewhere."

"There's a marker," Paulie says, pointing to a white post about 50 yards further along.

The track is narrow and leads up a dry watercourse between two hills. Very little plant life hangs on to these constantly eroding slopes, and deep ruts have been caused by rain and the runoff from melting snow.

"Looks like we've arrived on Mars," Paulie says.

You nod in agreement. "It's a strange landscape, alright."

The trail winds around one hill and then turns steeply uphill and runs along a broad ridge. "Look. There's the mine they mention in the guide."

Cut into the steep slope is a large hole framed by sturdy timbers. Near the entrance is an old pulley, some cable and other disused mining equipment. On its side is a beaten up wooden box with a steel undercarriage and wheels. Two railway tracks disappear into the hillside. To the left of the entrance, tumbling down the slope, is the pile of rubble discarded by the miners during their excavations.

"They must have used that railway to bring the dirt out," you say. "I wonder what they were searching for?"

Paulie pulls out his phone to take a picture. "Gold and silver most likely. Or maybe copper. There's also a lot of coal in Montana, but coal mines are usually big, ugly, open cast things, not underground mines like this."

"Where do you learn all this stuff, Paulie?" you say,

amazed. "Do you spend all your time on the internet?"

"Not really," he says. "I just remember things. And, I did some research before we came on this trip. I enjoy places more when I learn a bit about them beforehand."

"So do you think there's any gold left down there?" you ask.

Paulie shakes his head. "Not that we'd be able to find without some major equipment."

"What about fossils?"

"That's more likely," he says. "The miners probably weren't interested in those. They might have left a few lying around."

This sounds more interesting. You walk over and poke your head inside. "This shaft doesn't look very safe. These timbers are pretty old."

Fine dust drifts down from the roof. A few of the uprights have fallen onto the floor. You pull the flashlight out of your daypack and point it down the tunnel. About thirty yards in, you see a pile of huge bones.

Paulie sees them too. "Holy moly, are those dinosaur bones?"

You heart thumps with excitement. "Those bones are way too big to be anything else. Wow we've hit the mother lode."

"Wait," Paulie says, looking around nervously. "Who piled them up like that? Doesn't look like the work of miners."

"You're right. The miners would have dumped them

outside with all the other rubble."

As you're thinking about this mystery, the scrunch of footsteps comes from further down the path. Then, from around a corner, two men appear.

"Hey you brats! What do you think you're doing?" yells the larger of the two men.

"I don't think they're happy to see us, Paulie."

Paulie gasps. "They must be fossil smugglers. Look! He's got a pistol!"

"You two stay right there!" the man shouts.

"What do we do?" Paulie whispers.

"I don't know, but I'm not hanging around here. Quick! Run!"

But which way do you go? You can't go back the way you came, the men are blocking your way.

It looks like you only have two options. Do you:

Go into the deserted mine shaft? **P25**

Or

Follow the trail further up the hill? **P29**

You have decided to climb the arch.

You and Paulie run back along the path and waste no time climbing up the sandstone arch. Thankfully erosion, caused by the wind and rain, has provided you with plenty of handholds.

"What is that thing?" Paulie cries, his breath coming in short gasps as he climbs.

You're both puffing by the time you reach the top of the arch. As you catch your breath, you study the creature circling below. Its skin is a pale, scaly-green with tufts of red feathers on its elbows, head and tail. It walks on slim rear legs and has short forearms. Its big eyes look at you as if it thinks you'd make a nice lunch. The creature snaps up at you as it attempts to climb the arch, but its body isn't designed for climbing and despite the sharp talons on its hind legs, it skids back to the ground before making much upward progress.

Studying the beast, you pull out your guide book and flip through the pages. "I think it's a Troodon," you say. "But how could it be? They died out over 65 million years ago."

Paulie looks around and scratches his head. "Yeah I know. Only minutes ago, this place was almost desert. Now it's covered in plants and stuff. It's like we've traveled back to the Cretaceous period."

As bizarre as that sounds, how else could a dinosaur be pacing around beneath you? And how could so much of the Great Plains be covered in swampland?

Then you spot the meteorite lying on the ground far below and remember the strange humming. Could that have had something to do with all this? Did its vibrations open a portal to another dimension?

"This is so weird."

"It's a lot stranger than weird," Paulie says. "It's totally freaking me out."

The big lizard doesn't look like it's going anywhere. In fact, three of its friends have come to join it circling the arch. They look up at you, hiss, and make odd growling noises.

You sit down. "Well for the moment, I think I'll stay where I am. Those oversized reptiles look hungry. Look at the size of their teeth!"

"Did you know that Troodons were the smartest dinosaurs ever?" Paulie asks.

"How smart?" you ask nervously.

"A lot smarter than your average lizard, that's for sure. Dog smart maybe."

Thinking you may have quite a wait, you take off your daypack and pull out your water bottle. "Drink?" you say, offering the bottle to Paulie.

He shakes his head and sits down beside you. "How long do you think they'll hang around?"

"I don't know. More importantly, how long does it take an extremely smart lizard to learn how to climb?"

"Don't say that!" Paulie says, his eyes boring into yours.

Another hour passes. You both eat an energy bar.

When Paulie reaches for a second, you grab his arm. "We need to ration our food in case our new friends stick around."

"Not my fr–friends," Paulie says. Then his eyes widen and he turns his head slightly. He raises a hand to cup his ear. "Do you hear that?"

You listen hard for a moment. Then you hear it too. A low rumbling is coming from somewhere further down the ridge. It sounds like a lion's growl, only deeper, followed by something that sounds like an angry bull elephant calling. The Troodons hear it too. They screech nervously at each other and run about in confusion.

When the massive head of the T. Rex appears, you nearly poop yourself. You grab Paulie's sleeve. "Do you see what I see?"

"Holy moly!" Paulie says. "What do we do?"

The Troodons scuttle around looking for some way to escape, but they're trapped at the end of the ridge with steep cliffs all around. The T. Rex has cut them off and is moving towards them, its jaws snapping viciously from side to side. Drool flies from its mouth in a large arc, like a sprinkler watering a lawn. A few drops splatter the front of you.'

"Yuck! Dinosaur slobber," Paulie says in disgust. "Gross."

"Quick, lie down and stay still," you say. "In the movie *Jurassic Park* they said a T. Rex can't see you if you don't move."

Although Paulie does as you say, he shakes his head. "I

read somewhere that the movie got it wrong," he whispers.

"Thanks. Remind me to send Spielberg an email demanding an explanation if we get out of this."

"Did you know that Spielberg—"

"Paulie, be quiet! Let's just hope the T. Rex likes the taste of Troodon, better than people."

"But dinosaurs and humans didn't live in the same time period," Paulie says. "How would it know what people taste like?"

You shoot Paulie a scathing look and hold an index finger to your lips.

A growl from the T. Rex and another shower of drool makes you press yourselves down onto the rock of the arch. The dinosaur is bigger than you ever imagined. It stalks the Troodons, snapping left and right, as the much smaller, yet more agile dinosaurs try to sneak past it to safety. As one of the Troodon makes a desperate attempt to skitter past the T. Rex's position, the much bigger animal swivels its jaws and clamps on to the poor Troodon. A high-pitched screech echoes over the ridge.

As the T. Rex chews up the unlucky Troodon, the others take the opportunity to sprint past their unfortunate companion while the T. Rex's mouth is full. The last you see of them are their tails disappearing into the dense foliage.

With a swallow and a roar, the T. Rex spins around and takes off in pursuit.

"Do you think the T. Rex will come back?" Paulie asks, as if not quite believing what his eyes have witnessed. "Or should we make a run for it?"

Should you stay up on the arch or, like the Troodons, should you take this opportunity to get off the ridge?

It is time to make an important decision. Do you:

Stay on the arch? **P35**

Or

Get off the arch and off the ridge? **P42**

You have decided to go back into the canyon.

You start to run, but the ridge is narrow and the big lizard is blocking the path you came up. Skirting along the edge of the cliff, you search for another track down, but the canyon walls are far too steep for climbing. And even if you could get down, the once-dry canyon is filled with murky brown water.

Paulie panics beside you. "Let's jump into the water!"

"But how deep is it?" you ask. "And what's else is in there?"

"I don't know," Paulie says with terror in his eyes. "But we'd better do something or we'll end up being lizard lunch."

You look one way, then the other. "Back to the arch!"

"Hurry!" Paulie yells. "He's right behind us."

As you rush through the arch, you skid to a stop and duck to the right, behind one stone pillar. Paulie nips left.

In its eagerness to sink its teeth into you, the slobbering lizard is going way too fast to stop. With a final snap of its jaws and a scrabbling of hard claws on even harder rock, it skids right past and plummets over the edge and into the water below.

"Phew, that was close," you say, peering over the cliff to where the lizard is kicking hard, trying to stay afloat.

Neither you, nor the struggling Troodon, see the huge Tylosaurus coming, until it busts out of the water with the Troodon clamped in its massive jaws. Then, with a splash and a gurgle, both creatures disappear below the surface, leaving nothing but a series of ripples.

"Just as well we didn't go swimming eh, Paulie?"

Paulie stares at the water below. His knees wobble. "Please tell me this is a bad dream."

"Okay, it's all a horrible reptilian nightmare. You happy now?"

Paulie looks up at you. A tear rolls down his face. "But it isn't. Is it?"

You shake your head and give Paulie a pat on the shoulder. "No. And we need to figure out a way to get back home. Hang in there, we'll be okay."

Paulie does a 360 degree turn, his eyes searching, trying to make sense of it all. He sees his phone lying on the ground. "I wonder if that shot I took came out?"

"Have a look," you say. "It might give us a clue about what is going on."

He picks the phone up and starts scrolling though the images. "Here it is. Holy moly, look at this!"

He holds up the phone so you can see the screen. "Look at the rock in your hand!"

You peer at the screen. "That's right, the rock went bright red."

"Did it feel hot?" Paulie asks.

You shake your head. "Not really. And then the thing started making that horrible noise."

Paulie's left hand cradles his chin as he thinks. His eyes roll skyward. "That rock must have created a rip in the fabric of space-time somehow," he says.

Your upper lip rises as your face contorts. "Huh? Space-time?"

"Got a better explanation?"

You shrug. "No... Not really. Do you think it'll work in reverse?"

"Worth a try," he says. "Just one problem."

"What's that?"

"Well, if we go back in time, earth may not be here when we arrive. Remember our planet is moving through space."

"But what other option have we got?"

Paulie shrugs. "None that I can think of. We'll just have to hope space and time look after themselves."

You shake your head. "Well I'm pleased we've got the technical difficulties sorted." You pick up the meteorite and hold it out, willing it to turn red.

After a minute Paulie sighs. Nothing's happening." He looks at the photo again and a smile crosses his face. "The arch. We need to stand directly under the arch!"

You both move under Gabriel's Arch and, once again, stand expectantly with the rock held out. But still nothing happens.

You kick the ground and look over at Paulie. "Why isn't it working?"

Paulie shrugs. "I don't know. I'm not a physicist. Give it another minute."

Two minutes later it becomes obvious Paulie's theory is not going to work.

You look around. "Well I don't know about you, but I'd like to get off this ridge. I feel a bit trapped up here."

Paulie nods his agreement and points to a narrow track leading between a patch of ferns. "Let's head down there, eh? I can't see another path, can you?"

After putting the meteorite into your daypack, you head off, pulling fronds aside as you work your way down the ridge. You can hear Paulie's footsteps right behind you. Every twenty yards or so, you stop and listen for danger.

Paulie has his phone out, taking pictures.

As your ears strain trying to hear approaching dinosaurs, you hear a funny vibration coming from your daypack. "What's that?"

A blinding FLASH leaves you seeing spots.

"Yikes!" Paulie cries. "What the heck caused that!"

When your vision clears the jungle is gone. Once again the terrain around you is barren. If the jungle has gone, maybe the dinosaurs have too.

"Ar–are we back?" Paulie asks.

"The water is gone," you say looking over the canyon rim. "But I don't think we're back."

"Why do you say that?"

And then Paulie sees what you've seen. Bison. Not just one or two. But tens of thousands of them.

"What's going on?" he asks. "And where did all these bison come from?"

"I'm more interested in what caused that flash," you say. "Was it the meteorite again? Or something else?"

Paulie scrunches up his face as he tries to fathom out what is happening. "It must be the meteorite, but what's triggering it to flash like that? We know it wasn't the arch so what else could it be?" He looks down at his phone.

"What are you doing?" you ask him.

"I felt my phone vibrate just before the flash. Do you think that might have something to do with it? That's so weird, my phone only vibrates when I receive a text, but there's nothing."

"I hardly think there were cell phone towers in the Cretaceous period, Paulie."

Paulie looks a little hurt. "Yeah, but–"

"But what? You think text messages are going to zap us back and forth in time?"

Paulie shrugs. "I don't know what I think."

He looks about ready to cry. You move closer and put your arm over his shoulder. "Don't worry, we'll get back somehow. Hey, look on the bright side. How many kids get to go back in time? Imagine the school report we'll be able to write about our adventures!"

Paulie tries hard to smile. "Yeah, I suppose."

But what do you do now?

Head back to where your school group set up camp?**P54**

Or

Go back down into Gabriel's Gulch and keep exploring? **P59**

You have decided to go into the deserted mine shaft.

"Quick Paulie, in here."

You jump over a fallen support near the entrance of the shaft and rush deeper into the mine. As you pass the pile of bones, you see a couple of picks lying on the ground.

"Grab a pick for protection," you say, snagging one as you pass.

"Still no service." Paulie shoves his phone into a side-pocket of his pack, and grabs a pick. "We must be too far from the tower."

"Being underground won't help either," you say as you continue on.

Holding the flashlight, you work your way further into the mine. As you do, the support timbers look even less stable. The tunnel twists and turns. Side shafts branch off every fifteen yards or so. Some of them only go in for a few yards, others disappear into a darkness the powerful beam of your flashlight can't penetrate.

"Looks like the miners were following veins of ore," Paulie says. "There are tunnels all over the place."

The air down here is much cooler than outside. When you reach a large side shaft you turn to Paulie. "Let's see where this goes."

Paulie looks up at the cracked support timbers and frowns. "You sure this is a good idea?"

"Would you rather get caught by those men?"

Paulie shrugs. "Okay, let's go. Just be careful."

The next bones you pass are human. A skeleton, still dressed in tattered clothes, lies near the shaft. From its size you can tell it's an adult.

"Holy moly," Paulie says. "Its skull is cracked."

"It must be pretty old. Look at what it's wearing."

The pants, shirt and coat look like something you've seen in old photographs. With a shudder, you grab Paulie's sleeve. "Come on. Let's keep moving."

"We're gonna find you brats!" a voice echoes from the darkness behind you. The men sound quite a way back.

"Walk quietly," you whisper to Paulie. "We might be able to lose them."

The shaft slopes downward. You're careful not to trip over the rails running down the tunnel. But then, without warning, the rails disappear under a pile of rubble.

"There's be–been a cave-in," Paulie says. "Wha–what now?"

You shine your light over the pile of rubble. The roof has collapsed alright, but there is still a small gap between the pile and one of the walls. You feel a cool breeze.

"This tunnel must lead to the outside," you whisper. "I feel air coming through." You take your pick and start scraping at the loose rock. "Help me Paulie. We just need a hole big enough to squeeze through."

Unfortunately, it's hard to be quiet and dig at the same time.

"Work fast, they're bound to hear us," you say.

At least the rocks that have fallen are small enough to

shift. In less than a minute the hole looks big enough to squeeze through.

You shine your light into the gap. "You first, Paulie. Quick! They're coming!"

When another shaft of light flashes on the wall beside you, Paulie wastes no time in diving into the hole. You toss your flashlight after him and squeeze through. It's a tight fit, but you just manage to get through with only a few minor scrapes and scratches.

The men are close now. The scrunch of gravel grinds under their boots.

"Look, fresh prints," one of them says. "They must have wiggled through this hole."

A big hairy arm pokes a flashlight through the hole and illuminates you and Paulie. Then both of the men start laughing.

You turn to Paulie. "Why are they laughing?"

"Don't worry Walter," a gruff voice says. "Those brats aren't going anywhere."

After a moments silence, you hear thumping further back along the shaft. Then there's a splintering sound as one of the supports crashes onto the floor of the shaft.

Paulie grabs your arm. "I think they're trying to collapse the tunnel."

Paulie's suspicions are quickly confirmed when a low rumble shudders through the shaft and the sound of snapping timbers and a blast of dust and grit from falling rock shoots through the hole. When the cloud finally clears, you shine your light back towards the hole.

It's gone. All you can see is rubble.

"You okay, Paulie?" In the beam of the flashlight, damp lines run down Paulie's dirt-covered face. "Hey don't worry. Remember there was a breeze coming up this tunnel before those guys blocked it off. It must go back to the surface."

"It could be miles away. Maybe we should try to dig our way out. It could be dangerous going further in. What happens if our batteries run out while we're underground?"

Paulie has a point. Maybe digging your way out is the right plan. But then how are you to know how much rock has come down?

It is time to make a decision. Do you:

Go further down into the mine? **P97**

Or

Try to dig your way out? **P104**

You have decided to follow the trail up the hill.

"Quick, up here, Paulie!"

Without waiting for a reply, you start running up the track. When you look over your shoulder, Paulie is on your heels and the men are about 150 yards further down. There's a lot of loose rock on this part of the track. You try not to knock it down onto Paulie.

Uphill from your position, there's been a rock fall. A pile of stone lies across your path. Many of the stones are the size of softballs. You stop and heft one in your hand. It's heavy, with sharp edges.

Paulie stops beside you. "Are you thinking what I am?" he says, a grin crossing his face.

"Should give them second thoughts about chasing us," you say, flinging the rock down the slope towards the men.

Paulie picks up a rock and does the same.

As fast as you can, you throw rocks at the men.

"Hey you brats! I'm gonna–" The rest of his words are cut short as he dodges the missiles bouncing dangerously down the hill towards him.

Despite the men's curses, you and Paulie keep tossing rocks.

One of the men dodges left, then right, avoiding the rocks. His friend isn't so lucky and falls onto his back, clutching his leg and groaning. "Walter, help me. I think I've broken my leg."

"Let's go," you say. "I don't think they'll be following us

anymore."

Paulie drops the rock in his hand. "So, what now?"

"We need to get back to camp and tell the park rangers there are smugglers up here."

Paulie looks down towards the men. "But they're on the path."

"We'll have to find another way," you say. "Come on, we don't want to be out here after dark."

Without further delay, you and Paulie head up the hill.

Once you've put a bit of distance between you and the smugglers, you stop climbing and pull out your guide. "This map isn't very detailed, but I think this trail leads around the hill to a spring at the head of another canyon."

Paulie pulls his water bottle out of his pack and takes a slug. "A spring, that's good. My water's getting low."

The ground is rugged. Eroded channels streak the hillside, cutting across the path in places. Rain has washed a lot of soil away. In the distance, pinnacles point towards the sky, all that is left of once-mighty hills.

"What the heck?" Paulie says as you come around a corner. He points towards a dusty old trailer, its hitch propped up on a lump of sandstone. "How did that get up here?"

You look around expecting to see a dirt track. But Paulie's right. There's no road, just the narrow track you're on. Outside the trailer sits an old lawn chair and a barbeque. Whisky bottles and tin cans litter the ground around the chair. As you survey the camp, you notice a big eye-ring bolted to each corner of the trailer's chassis. One still has a length of rusty chain attached to it. "It must have been lifted it in by helicopter. See those ring thingies?"

Paulie looks confused. "But why here?"

"I don't know. Survivalists maybe? Fossil hunters?"

"What if they're friends with those men?" Paulie asks.

You shrug. "I suppose it's possible … but this trailer looks like it's been here for years. I doubt the smugglers have been operating that long. Surely someone would have seen them."

The raggedy curtain in one of the windows twitches. You grab hold of Paulie's elbow, turn your back to the trailer, and pretend to look at the view. "Don't look now, Paulie," you whisper, "but someone's watching us."

"Wha–what do we do?" he asks

"They could be friendly."

"Or they could have a shotgun." Paulie shakes your hand off. "Let's get the heck out of here."

You're about to agree when the trailer door creaks open and an old-timer with a long white beard, flannel shirt and tattered trousers peers out at you. He steps down from inside clutching a walking stick in one hand.

"What're you two young'uns doing way up here? Not looking for gold I hope."

Deciding to play it cagey you don't mention the two smugglers. "Nah, we're on a school trip. Just out for a walk. The rest of the class should be along soon."

The old man scratches his chin. "Long as you don't do no

prospecting. I've got claim to this here piece o' dirt."

Then you have an idea. "Have you seen any bones lying around?"

"Bones? Now why would I want bones? I'm looking for Bill Rafferty's hidden…" He scowls at you. "You sure you're not lookin' for Rafferty's treasure?"

Paulie suddenly takes an interest. "Is that the prospector that went missing in 1863?"

"So you are claim jumpers!" the old man yells.

Paulie shakes his head. "No, no, I just read about it on the internet. Didn't Rafferty strike it rich in Willard Creek?"

The old man seems unsure for a moment, then he looks you both up and down, realizes you're just harmless kids, and smiles, showing a gap in his front teeth. "Lewis and Clark named it Willard creek when they passed by in the early 1800s. But when a plague of grasshoppers came through in '62 they renamed it Grasshopper Creek."

"That's right," Paulie says. "Wasn't the gold unusually pure?"

The old man nods. "Ninety nine percent they reckon. You got a good memory there, kiddo. I've been lookin' for that gold nigh on forty years. Not found a single nugget. But I will, just you watch. Long as this wonky knee don't give out on me."

"Well good luck," you say. "I don't suppose you could point us towards the campsite at Gabriel's Gulch? We need to get back before dark and report some smugglers we saw further down."

"Smugglers eh?" the old man says. "Those varmints better stay off my patch, or I'll give 'em what for." The old man takes a few practice swings with his cane, pretending it's a sword, before pointing up the hill with it. "See that ridge. Well, over that is the top o' Long Canyon. It's narrow, but once you work your way along, you'll come to a spring, then you just need to follow the creek bed down to the flat. Should be able to see your camp from there."

"Thanks Mister," you say, grabbing Paulie's arm and dragging him along before he starts asking the man more questions.

"Oh and if you're interested," the old guy says, "there's some big bones near the bottom of Long Canyon. Look along the north wall. I ran across a paleontologist once a few years back, said they was an Eino … um … Eino something or other bones."

"Einiosaurus?" Paulie says.

The old man nods. "Yes'um, that's it."

Paulie smiles and turns to you. "They're like a Triceratops, only smaller."

"Those big ones with the three horns and bony collar?" you ask.

Paulie nods. "That's the one."

"Just a pile o' bones to me," the old man grumbles. "You're welcome to all the bones you like, just leave my gold alone or you'll have me to answer to."

You wave goodbye. "Hope your knee holds up, Mister. Good luck."

With that, you and Paulie continue your trudge uphill. At least the sun is lower in the sky and the heat of the day is lessening. When you finally reach the ridge, you stop and take in the view.

"Wow, look at that," Paulie says.

Far below, water has cut a deep scar across the landscape. Layers of red, brown, orange, tan and yellow strike through the hills. Pinnacles of harder sandstone have been left standing, and the wind and rain have carved many unusual shapes out what were once solid mountains.

There are a couple of ways down to the canyon floor from here. You could go along the ridge, which is more gently sloping. Or you could take a more direct route down one of the many watercourses.

It is time to make a decision. Do you:

Follow the ridge? **P49**

Or

Go down a watercourse? **P75**

You have decided to stay on the arch.

A slight breeze blows across your sweaty skin as you sit atop the arch. "With so many dinosaurs around, maybe we should stay up here until dark," you say to Paulie. "We can't afford to be caught in the open."

Paulie looks like he's about to cry. His lower lip quivers and his eyes dart left and right as if expecting a new danger to show itself at any moment.

"Hey, don't worry," you say, trying not to expose your fear to your younger companion. "We'll make it out of this."

"Oh yeah. How is that?"

"Hey we've got bigger brains than those lizards. We just need to make a plan."

Paulie exhales a long slow breath, then sniffs. "I'm glad you're so confident." He pulls his knees in tight to his chest and wraps his arms around them before closing his eyes.

Paulie looks pale and his breathing is coming in rapid gasps as he rocks back and forth. You place your hand on his arm. His skin is cool and clammy despite the warmth of the afternoon. This does not look good.

"I think you're going into shock, Paulie. Lie down on your back and rest your feet on my lap."

Paulie opens his eyes and looks at you. His pupils are enlarged. Another bad sign. But at least he does as you say and lays on his back and elevates his feet. You pull your extra sweatshirt out of your daypack and lay it over him.

Down the valley, you hear the screech of Troodons and

wonder if the T. Rex has cornered them.

The sun is getting low in the sky, and grey clouds are rolling in from the north. After twenty minutes or so, Paulie's breathing has settled and the color has returned to his face.

Further down the canyon you hear the sound of running water – a stream or waterfall perhaps. Every now and then there is a big splash, and you make a note not to go in the water without good reason. Who knows what creatures lurk below its surface?

Paulie opens his eyes. His pupils are back to normal. "I'm feeling better now," he says. "I thought I was going to puke there for a moment." He sits up and reaches for his water bottle. After a long drink and a look around he opens the front pouch of his daypack and pulls out a chocolate bar. "Want some?"

As the two of you munch on the chocolate, you discuss your options.

"We need to figure out what caused us to time-jump," Paulie says. "Then figure out how to do it again, but in reverse."

What he says makes sense.

"It's got to be that meteorite," you say. "What else could have caused it?"

Paulie pulls an ear as he thinks. "Maybe. But meteorites don't usually cause time travel so there must be something else to it as well. Some interaction we don't understand."

Then, Paulie sees his phone still sitting on the rock where he put it to take the picture. "The phone … it must be the phone!"

"You think so?"

He clutches your arm. "One of us needs to climb down and get the meteorite and the phone."

You can see the fear in his eyes and the last thing you want is for him to go back into shock. "I'll go," you say. "But you keep watch. Call out the moment you see anything coming. Okay?"

Paulie nods enthusiastically. "Will do."

Climbing down is always trickier than climbing up because it's harder to see where to put your feet. Much of the time your feet are swinging in thin air trying to find the next hole. Your arms ache by the time you get to the bottom and sweat runs down your back in the hot, sticky air.

You walk quickly over to the phone and put it in your front pocket. Then you pick up the meteorite. The rock looks normal again. Not a hint of red anywhere. "Hmmm." You stuff it into your back pocket and look up towards Paulie on the arch.

When a large shadow moves across the ground in front of you, at first you think it's Paulie's. But then you realize the sun is in the wrong position for that to be the case. You swivel around and scan the sky. Then you see the flying lizard. It's a Pterodactyl.

The strange beast has a thin membrane of skin stretched between its elongated front arms and its rear legs to form a wingspan of about nine feet. Its head is like that of a deformed goose, with a long orange beak containing rows of small teeth.

"Watch out!" you yell.

Paulie sees the Pterodactyl just in time and ducks, but not before the creature has knocked him off balance. "Whooooa!" he yells, teetering on the edge.

Things happen in slow motion. Paulie is falling. Without thinking, you position yourself to catch him, stretching your arms out as his frame fills the sky above you.

"Umphhhh," you grunt as you hit the ground with Paulie on top of you.

"You okay, Paulie?" Untangling yourself, you sit up and check for injuries. A large graze down your leg oozes blood. Your ribs hurt. But otherwise, you've been lucky not to be more severely injured.

Paulie rubs his hip where he landed. He has a raw patch near his elbow, but as he gets up, you see he's okay.

Another shadow flashes across the ground, then another. This time you both know where it's coming from and scan the sky.

"Quick! Under the arch!" you say, scrambling to your feet.

Paulie wastes no time following you. When you look up again you see three Pterodactyls, circling above, like vultures.

"We need to get the heck out of here," Paulie says. "Give me my phone. Let me see if I can work out what happened."

Pleased to see that the phone wasn't damaged in your tumble, you pass it over. "No rush, Paulie. Anytime in the next minute or so should be fine."

Your backside is a bit sore where you thumped down hard on the meteorite. You pull the rock out of your pocket as Paulie fiddles with his phone. Then unexpectedly, after Paulie has switched the phone off and then restarted it, the meteorite starts to vibrate and turn red.

"Something's happening!" you say, one eye on the rock and the other on the circling dinosaurs above.

Then, with a FLASH, the Pterodactyls are gone … and so is the jungle.

All seems normal again. "Hey, Paulie, I think we're back."

"Look again," Paulie says, his eyes wide as he looks through the arch towards the flatland beyond the canyon.

"But–" Then you see what Paulie is referring to. Along the base of the hills, in the distance, is a raised track. Running along that single rail is a sleek train moving at incredible speed.

"That certainly wasn't there when we came into the canyon," Paulie says. "It's like that fast train in Japan–"

"The bullet train?"

"Yeah, but look at it go! It must be doing five hundred miles an hour!"

You and Paulie sit down under the arch and look out over the landscape. Further down the valley are a pair of gleaming towers. As the train approaches them, it quickly slows, then stops altogether.

"Is that a train station?" Paulie asks.

"Dunno. Those towers must be 100 stories high."

"Maybe it's a town?"

You scratch your head. "Not like any town I've ever seen. But I suppose we should go and check it out. They might help us find a way home."

After cleaning up your scrapes and scratches, you head towards the towers. It takes about an hour before you can see them more clearly.

"I see a sign," Paulie says, pulling a pair of binoculars out of his daypack.

"What's it say?"

Paulie starts laughing. "You're not going to believe this." He hands you the binoculars.

You hold them up to your eyes and peer through the lenses. Twiddling the dial, you bring the sign into focus. It reads: WELCOME TO GABRIEL'S GULCH WORLD WILDLIFE HOTEL

"Looks like we jumped a bit too far," you say.

"Yeah, but won't it be interesting!" Paulie is bobbing up and down like a jack-in-the-box. "Did you know that Einstein said…"

You ignore Paulie's ramblings as you wander towards the hotel. The sky is crystal blue and cloudless. The air smells pure and clean. Maybe the people of earth finally got their act together and stopped the pollution and the damages due to climate change. Maybe things are different now. You sure hope so.

"Hey, Paulie," you say. "Can I borrow those binoculars again?"

He digs in his pack. "Sure."

Then you see what you're looking for. It's another sign just beside the entrance to the hotel. It reads:

FREE ICE CREAM FOR CHILDREN UNDER 18

"Hey, Paulie."

"Yeah?"

"I think we're going to like the future."

"You think so?"

You're grinning so hard your face hurts. "Yeah. I'm sure of it."

Congratulation you've finished this part of the story. What would you like to do now?

Go back to the beginning of the story and try a different path? **P1**

Or

Go to the list of choices and start reading from another part of the story? **P136**

You say which way!

42

You have decided to get off the arch.

"We've been up here long enough," you say. "We need to figure out how to get home."

"Did you know that Einstein predicted that man might be able to go forward in time, but never backward?"

"Well we've proven him wrong, haven't we? Remind me to write up the mathematical equation for it when we get back to camp."

Paulie looks puzzled. "The mathematical equation?"

You give him a smile. "I'm joking, numbskull."

"Oh," Paulie says, his face reddening.

You spin around onto your stomach and start climbing down the arch. "Now stop talking about Einstein and help me figure out a way to get home. Oh, and keep an eye out for those lizards."

Back on the ground, you pick up the meteorite. "This rock must have something to do with what happened. Did you see how it turned red and vibrated before it flashed?"

Paulie nods. "And the sound it made. What was that all about?"

You shrug. "Alien folk music?"

"Not funny," Paulie says rolling his eyes. He picks up his phone from the rock and slides it into his pocket. "So, what now?"

"Well normally if you get lost, you're meant to stay put and wait to be rescued. But I doubt anyone will even miss us for a few hours."

"Not to mention the 65 million year time difference," Paulie says.

"Yeah, and that."

Paulie sits on a rock and closes his eyes. It is a pose you've seen him take many times over the last couple of hours. His thinking pose. You've been doing a fair bit of thinking yourself. Trying to remember exactly how you found yourselves in this situation.

"Have you heard of meridians, Paulie?"

Paulie opens his eyes. "You mean spots on the earth that have some sort of mystical energy?"

"Yeah I remember reading about them somewhere. Could that be the cause of our jump?"

"It's possible," Paulie says. "It also possible that little green spacemen or the cookie monster did it. Extremely unlikely, but within the realm of possibility."

"Yes, but–"

"Have you heard of Occam's razor?" Paulie asks.

"What's shaving got to do with it?"

"No, it's nothing to do with shaving. It's just the principal that a simple explanation is more likely to be correct than a complicated one."

"Such as?"

"Like UFOs for example. A simple explanation for weird lights in the sky could be that it's something earth-based – a plane or balloon – or some unusual atmospheric condition."

You nod. "Okay."

"A complicated explanation would be that aliens have

made a spacecraft capable of travelling hundreds, or millions of light years and they've managed to find earth amongst the millions of billions of planets out there in the universe. Oh, and then they leave again without bothering to say hello properly."

"I see what you mean. So simple is good."

"Yes."

"So, what's the simple explanation for us time jumping?"

"Well, let's just say, it's probably something less complicated than some wacky notion of invisible meridians that science has never detected."

You can see where Paulie is headed. "Okay, so the simplest explanation is that it's something to do with either the phone, the arch, or the meteorite?"

"Exactly." He pulls his phone out of his pocket and looks at it. "I can't see anything strange going on with my phone. Except that there's no reception."

"Well that's hardly surprising. I'd be pretty shocked to discover dinosaurs had cell phone towers."

But when Paulie's phone make a loud DING indicating he's just received a text, you both stare down at it.

"How is that possible?" you ask.

Paulie hits the key pad and peers at the screen.

You watch as Paulie's eyes widen and jaw drops. Then he brings the phone closer to his face, as if looking at it closer will change the message somehow. "Bu–but that's imposs–impossible."

"Come on. Tell me. What's it say?"

Paulie shudders like something's sent a chill through him. "It's a message from the future."

"From who?" you say, leaning forward, trying to catch a glimpse of the screen.

He holds up from the screen. "From me in 2060!"

The message reads:

> MAY 2060: YOU CAN GET
> HOME BY REBOOTING YOUR
> PHONE WHILE HOLDING IT
> NEAR THE METEORITE.
> PAUL LEIGHTON SMITH.

"But that's over 40 years from now!"

Finding yourself back in the Cretaceous period with the dinosaurs was strange enough, but messages from the future? That's totally weird.

"Yeah, isn't it great?" Paulie has a big smile on his face. "Don't you see, for me to be sending messages from the future, we must survive!"

You think about what he's said for a moment, then turn and look directly at him. "We?" you say. "Is my name on the text too?"

The smile drops from his face. "Sorry, I just assumed…"

"Yeah well don't! Just get moving with the phone. I want to get home. Now would be good, before that hungry T. Rex returns!"

Paulie wastes no time turning off his phone. You hold out the meteorite in the palm of your hand as he turns his phone back on. Both of you stare at the screen as you wait for it to come to life.

The rock in your hand has just started to vibrate when there is crashing through the jungle nearby. It sounds like it's coming right towards you.

"Hurry up, phone!" you yell at the piece of plastic in Paulie's hand. "That sounds like Mister T. Rex, and he's moving fast!

The animal's massive head pokes above the nearby bushes and you nearly pee. The T. Rex growls, low and mean, then stretches its neck towards you just as the vibrating meteorite starts its high-pitched screeching. The T. Rex snaps its head back, raises it to the sky and lets out a massive roar.

"I don't think it likes that squeal," you yell to Paulie.

FLASH!

"Are we back?" Paulie says, looking around.

The jungle is gone and the much sparser scrubland of sagebrush, gumweed and various grasses is back. A lizard skitters along the ground. Thankfully, this one is only a few inches long.

"I think so," you say. "Come on, let's head back to camp and find out."

The two of you waste no time walking back down Gabriel's Gulch. A red-tailed hawk flies high overhead looking for prey. Then, as a jackrabbit darts across a bare patch of land a few yards away, the hawk dives, only to have the rabbit disappear down a hole moments before it can get its razor-sharp talons onto it. Life and death on the badlands goes on. Only the hunters have changed.

"Who'd want to be lunch eh, Paulie?"

"We nearly were!"

You have never been so pleased to see a clump of pup-tents in your life. "Phew, Paulie," you say with relief. "Looks like you're a hero."

"Me?" he says. "How do you figure that?"

"Not you now. You as an old man in 2060. You saved us from that T. Rex. If we hadn't got that text, we would have been eaten."

Paulie stands taller. His chest puffs out. "Yeah, I guess I am ... I mean will be. But how did that work without us having any cell phone reception?"

You shrug. "That, my friend, is a very good question."

Paulie turns to you and smiles. "I wonder if we're still friends in 2060? Maybe you and I work out how to time travel. You've still got that meteorite, don't you?"

It's then that you realize the meteorite is no longer in your hand. "Where is it?" You pat your pockets, looking around at the ground."

You are so focused on finding the piece of space rock that you jump when Paulie's phone goes off.

"Who's that?" you ask.

Paulie hits a button on his keypad and reads the message.

"It's from me again."

"Really? What's it say?"

Paulie laughs. "Here, read it yourself."

MAY 2060: I HAVE HIDDEN

THE METEORITE. YOU
WON'T FIND IT UNTIL YOU
ARE A FEW YEARS OLDER
AND MORE RESPONSIBLE. IN
THE MEANTIME, STUDY
PHYSICS. YOU TWO ARE
GOING TO BE FAMOUS …
JUST NOT FOR A FEW YEARS
YET. HAVE FUN IN THE
MEANTIME. PAUL LEIGHTON
SMITH.   (PHD)

Congratulations: This part of your story is over. You and Paulie have survived an encounter with a T. Rex. And, it sounds like you both have bright futures.

So, what would you like to do now? Do you:

Go back to the start and read a different path? **P1**

Or

Go to the list of choices and start reading from somewhere else in the book? **P136**

You have decided to follow the ridge.

"So, bones in the canyon eh?" Paulie says.

"That's what the old guy said. Assuming they're still there."

Paulie speeds up and takes the lead, "Only one way to find out."

Walking down the ridge is easy going. With all the amazing scenery to take in, it doesn't seem long before you're standing at the bottom. The canyon is wider here than further up, but the layers in the rock are still plainly visible.

"Now to find these bones." Paulie's head turns left, then right.

"But shouldn't we be getting back to camp to report those men?"

"Of course. Duh," Paulie says, smacking himself on the forehead. "I almost forgot about them."

You smile. "I suppose we can look as we go … can't do any harm, can it?"

"Sounds like a plan."

"If we pick a side of the canyon each, we can cover more ground," you say. "You take this side, and I'll go over and scout the other. But we can't waste too much time, so keep moving."

Paulie agrees. You walk the twenty yards or so to the other side of the canyon. The layers of rock are very interesting. Some are only a few inches thick, while others are a yard or more. Each layer represents a period of time. Now you just need to figure out which one is the right time for dinosaurs.

Across the canyon, Paulie is facing the rock wall as he walks. Every now and again, he stops and picks up a rock, or pokes at the rock face.

You're so busy watching your friend that you don't see the rotten timbers on the ground in front of you until it's too late and the planks are cracking under your feet.

"Yeowwwwww!" you yell as you crash through a trap door and start to fall.

Paulie's head snaps around just before you disappear.

Luckily, quite a bit of sand has drifted through the cracks over time and piled up at the bottom of the hole to break your fall. As you pick yourself up and dust yourself off, your eyes adjust to the gloom. Off the main pit, someone has dug a narrow chamber back into the rock under the canyon wall."

"You okay down there?" Paulie yells.

"Yeah, thanks to the sand." Then, through the gloom, you see an old wooden trunk. "There's something down here!"

"Not rattlesnakes, I hope."

You hadn't thought about snakes. You reach into your pack, pull out your flashlight and scan the hole for reptiles. Thankfully there are no snakes, just an old ladder leaning against the wall.

"No snakes," you yell up to Paulie. "But there is an old

trunk."

Paulie's head pops over the edge and he peers down. "A treasure chest with Rafferty carved in its top, perhaps?"

"Not that I can see." You undo the clasp and lift the lid. "Here goes…"

"What's in it?" say Paulie. "Don't keep me in suspenders!"

"Nothing!" you grump. "Filthy things's empty, apart from a piece of paper."

"Empty? You're joking."

Disappointed, you reach down and pick up the sheet of paper. It looks like a map, but you're not sure. You sigh and tuck the note into your back pocket. After climbing back up to the surface, you take the note out and hand it to Paulie. "Here, have a look."

Paulie looks at the paper, rotates it around and then starts laughing. "You know what this means don't you?"

"No. What?"

"It's a map to Rafferty's treasure! See here. X marks the spot. And this faded writing says William Rafferty."

"Okay, so it's his map. But where the heck is X?" you ask.

"Remember that old stone wall in the campground?"

"The one by the camp kitchen?"

Paulie and you stare at each other a moment. "Shaped like an X," the two of you say in unison.

You give Paulie a grin. "So we were camped right beside the treasure all along?"

"That's my guess," Paulie says. "Only one way to be

sure."

And with that, you forget all about fossils and head back towards camp.

About halfway to camp, Paulie's phone beeps. He pulls it out of his pocket. "We must be back in range." He shades it from the sun so he can read the screen. "It's from a friend wishing me luck finding fossils."

"Hey, while you've got a signal. Call the police and tell them about the smugglers."

Half an hour later, after speaking to the police, and as the sun sets behind the hills, you stroll into camp. The old stone wall looks more like an X from this angle. Next to the wall, you find various parents sitting around the table, talking and preparing the evening meal. Mister Jackson looks up from chopping onions and gives you a funny look. "What are you two so happy about? You're grinning like you've won the lottery."

"Grab a shovel, Mister J, and we'll show you."

"Show me what?"

You shake your head. "Nah. I'm not going to say. That would spoil all the fun."

The next day, all the kids call you the "prairie dogs" as you dig around the old wall. It doesn't help that you haven't told them why. The first time you ask Mister Jackson to move the camp kitchen, he lightheartedly complies. The second time, he decides enough is enough.

Then, just as you're about to get a telling off, Paulie's shovel rings out against something metal.

"Holy moly," he says. "I think I've found it!"

Congratulations, that is the end of this part of your story. But have you followed all the different paths the story takes? It is time to make another decision. Do you:

Go back to the beginning and try a different path? **P1**

Or

Go to the list of choices and read from another part of the story? **P136**

(The list of choices is also a good place to check to make sure you haven't missed parts of the story.)

Head back to where your school group set up camp.

"I think we should head back to camp," you say. "At least that way if there's another flash, we can tell if we're back in the right time or not."

Paulie nods. "Okay with me, assuming we don't spook the bison and start a stampede."

He has a point. There are so many animals out there, who knows how they'll react to seeing people.

You and Paulie follow the ridge until you get to a point where you can descend back into the canyon. From this vantage point you can see a long way. On the far side of the canyon the Great Plains stretch out for miles in all directions. Countless bison graze on the lush grassland.

Feeling more relaxed, you study the amazing sight. At least bison, being herbivores, aren't going to eat you.

Paulie looks less frightened too. "Hey," he says. "Did you know that there were more than 20 million bison grazing on the Great Plains at one time?"

Considering how many you can see right now, you're not at all surprised.

"And over 40 different bird species lived here."

Yup, Paulie's back to normal, alright.

"Come on," you say. "We'd better make tracks."

But Paulie's on a roll. "Oh and prairie dogs and pronghorn lived here too," he says. "Still do."

"Pronghorns?" you say over your shoulder. "What are they when they're at home?"

"Relatives of the antelope," he says. "They're the fastest land animal in all of North America and second fastest in the whole world, after the cheetah."

"You obviously haven't seen me being chased by that nasty dog that lives down my street."

"I doubt you hit 60 miles an hour, somehow," Paulie says with a grin. "Pronghorns run fast enough to merge with freeway traffic."

"Beep, beep!" you say, speeding up. "Just watch me!"

The canyon floor looks much the same as it did when you first arrived, before the episode with the Troodons and T. Rex. Still, you scan the area just to be sure there are no gigantic reptiles hanging around waiting for lunch to wander by.

Paulie sees your nervous looks. "Don't worry, dinosaurs were extinct well before the rise of big mammals like bison."

You feel a little better, but only for a second.

"But there might be mountain lions around," Paulie says, "so keep your eyes peeled."

High above you, on the ridge, you see the arch. The sun glints off its surface. It looks pretty much the same as before you were taken back to the Cretaceous era, maybe a little bigger and thicker, but not by much. You turn your back on the arch and start hoofing it back to where camp would be, if only you were in the right time, keeping an eye on the terrain around you as you go.

"So what do we do once we get to the campsite?" Paulie asks.

"We try to figure out what made us time jump."

"And if we can't figure it out?" Paulie's looking a bit agitated again. "How will we survive out here on our own?"

"I'm sure it won't come to that," you say, trying to sound confident. "Besides, there's a trillion bison burgers within a mile of where we're standing."

Paulie gives you a funny look. "Yeah, we'd just need to figure out how to catch them … and make fire to cook them … and grind wild wheat to make buns for them to go on."

You pull a box of matches from your daypack and give them a shake. "Would you like fries with that?"

But Paulie's having none of it, "Sorry, no potatoes around here. They originated in South America. Peru or Bolivia, I seem to recall."

"What about corn, then?" you say. "We could make tortillas."

Paulie shakes his head. "Corn comes from central Mexico. That's quite some walk from here, I'm afraid."

By the time Paulie stops telling you where all his favorite foods come from, you are out of Gabriel's Gulch and heading across the flat land towards where the campsite should have been.

Fifteen minutes later you stop. "I reckon this is the spot."

Paulie looks around. There is nothing but sagebrush. "Okay, now what?" he says, dumping his bag on the ground. "All that talk of food's made me hungry."

"We need to figure out what made us leap back in time," you say, pulling the meteorite out of your daypack. "It must have something to do with this rock."

Paulie's face is twisted in confusion. "But how?"

You've been mulling over this problem on the walk back. "Paulie, where's your phone?"

"My phone? What's that got to–"

You sigh and hold out your hand. "Just give it to me."

"Okay, okay. Don't blow a foo-foo valve." Paulie grabs his phone and passes it to you. "So what are you going to do?"

You turn the phone off. "I have an idea." Once it's powered down, you turn it on again while holding the rock nearby.

Paulie stares for a moment and then his eyes widen. "So you think something to do with the phone's electromagnetic radiation has reacted with the meteorite to alter the space time continuum? Seems a bit of a stretch."

"Got a better idea?"

He shrugs and shakes his head. "Where's a physicist when you need one, eh?"

You're not all that hopeful that the phone is the cause, but then, as the phone lights up, you feel a tingling in the palm of your hand. At first you think it's just the phone's vibrate function, but the rock is getting warm as well. "Something's happening!"

The rock starts to glow. A few moments later, it looks red hot, but you have no problem holding it in your hand.

"It's working!" Paulie says in excitement, but then he looks confused. "But how?"

"If I knew I'd tell you. Let's just hope it gets us back to the right time."

As the vibrations increase, Paulie inches away from you. His eyes are wide, with white showing all around his pupils. "Holy moly…"

"Move closer!" you say. "You don't want to be left behind do you?"

Just as Paulie takes a step in your direction, there is a blinding flash.

As the smoke clears you see tents and classmates.

"Where did you two sneak up from?" says Mr. Jackson from ten paces away. "And where did you get the fireworks? You know they're not allowed on school trips."

Paulie's in shock. His mouth is hanging open and there is a smudge of soot on his cheek.

Mr. Jackson's hands are on his hips. His eyes bore into you. "Well, are you going to answer me?"

But how do you explain what just happened? And would Mister Jackson believe you if you tried? You look at Paulie. He's lost for words, his mouth is moving, but nothing's coming out.

So what do you do? Do you:

Try to explain the time travel to Mister Jackson? **P88**

Or:

Keep the secret to yourself? **P81**

You have decided to explore further up Gabriel's Gulch.

When you reach the bottom of the gulch you see a fast-moving stream running through its center. The water looks clean and cool as it races through a narrow channel in the rock, worn smooth over time.

"We should fill up our water bottles," Paulie says. "Just in case we have to leave the canyon in a hurry."

You nod. "Good idea."

With bottles filled, you work your way further upstream. You can hear the sound of Bison grazing on the prairie above the canyon rim. Around one corner you come across a carcass lying on the floor of the canyon.

Paulie look up the steep canyon wall. "This bison's gone base jumping without a parachute." He kicks one of the huge horns protruding from the animal's head.

"Don't touch it," you say. "It'll have germs all over it."

Paulie crouches down and studies the dead bison. "I'm not worried about germs so much," he says, poking at some deep scratches in the animal's hide with his finger. "I–I'm worried about what's been eating this."

"What could it be?" you ask.

"Wolves maybe," he says, "or a mountain lion?"

"Maybe we should head back." A tingle of fear runs down your back. "I don't mind bison or pronghorns, but wolves…"

A deep snarl echoes through the canyon. Your stomach lurches as you scan for the animal that made it.

Paulie leaps up and looks around nervously. "You see it?"

Then you spot the big cat against the canyon wall. Its tawny coat blends in with the surroundings perfectly. Only the white patches on the cat's chest, cheeks and mouth stands out against the sandstone.

You lift an arm and point. "There."

"Uh oh." Paulie clutches your arm. "It must think we're after its meal."

You search for an escape route. "Back up slowly, Paulie. Angle towards the water."

Your eyes never leave the cat as it slowly creeps toward you. A dozen or so steps and you are on the edge of the quickly moving stream.

"I hope big cats don't like to swim," you say.

As the cat moves forward, you and Paulie walk backwards along the bank.

Then with a sudden rush, the mountain lion is sprinting flat out right at you! You hook your arm into Paulie's and leap.

In an instant you're sliding along the well-worn channel. You struggle to straighten up and point your feet downstream. The powerful current pushes into your back, moving you faster and faster along the slippery rock.

Paulie's arm tightens on yours.

You take a quick glance over your shoulder. The confused cat is almost fifty yards back, standing by the channel where you entered. The danger has passed. For now at least.

"Yippee! This is like a big slippery slide!" you yell.

But Paulie's face is twisted into a grimace rather than a smile.

"Come on, Paulie, enjoy the ride while it lasts."

Paulie grits his teeth and shakes his head. "Did you know that most fast moving streams end in waterfalls?" he says.

"You just made that up!" you shout over the sound of rushing water.

"So what's that then?" he says, pointing with his free arm.

Paulie's right. Thirty yards further down, the stream disappears over a lip.

"Yikes! How far will the drop be?" you ask.

"How should I know!"

You let go of Paulie's arm and try to climb up the channel walls, but it's useless. The rock is far too slick to get a hold on, and the force of the water is too strong to fight. You have no option. You're going over the edge whether you want to or not.

Paulie is doing windmills as he furiously back-paddles in a useless attempt to slow his progress towards the edge.

You fly over the lip of the falls and plunge towards a deep pool at the bottom. Thankfully, rather than there being rock, it's more like jumping off the high platform of your local pool.

With a SPLASH, you hit the water. You dogpaddle over to a low bank on one side, climb out of the water and up into a patch of sun. After slipping your daypack off, you look back towards your friend. "You okay, Paulie?"

Paulie is lying on the edge of the pool shivering. After a

moment, he climbs up to join you. "Now I know why I prefer books. Real life is scary."

"Don't people say, what doesn't kill you makes you stronger?" you say, with a grin. "Wow, what a ride."

Paulie looks over and scowls. "Do you really believe that? I was nearly maimed. How would that have made me stronger?"

You start to reply, but then notice Paulie has taken his phone out and is giving it a shake.

"Is it still working?" you ask.

"It should be alright," he says. "I've got a waterproof cover on it. But there's only one way to find out. I'll be angry if I've lost all my photos."

As Paulie fiddles with his phone, you sit on the smooth sandstone and warm up. Steam rises from your clothes as they dry.

"Okay, here goes," Paulie says about to push the 'on' button.

"Hey, wait a minute," you say. "Look at that!"

Distracted from his phone, Paulie looks up to where you're pointing. The end of a large bone is poking out of the crumbling canyon wall. Paulie stares at the bone like he's trying to burn a hole in it with his eyes. Then, after a minute, he looks over at you. "Is that what I think it is?"

"Well, if you think it's a ginormous dinosaur bone, I think you're right. Look at the size of it!"

Both of you leap up and rush over to the bone protruding out of the cliff.

"That's huge," Paulie says rubbing his hand along fossil.

"If this were a chicken leg," you say tugging on one end it, "the chicken would have to have been twenty feet tall. Give me a hand, Paulie, it feels loose."

The next few minutes are spent wiggling the bone left then right, gradually working it out of its resting place for the last 65 million years or so.

"I don't think it's big enough to be a bone from a T. Rex," Paulie says, "but it's way too big to be a bison."

When the bone finally lets go, you lurch back and fall on your backside. The bone, all five feet of it, drops to the ground in front of you.

You wipe your sleeve across your forehead. "Phew, that was hard work."

"Holy moly," Paulie says, looking at the bone on the ground in front of him, "what a good score."

"Yeah, I can't wait to show Mister J…" you say before realizing you're still in another time.

"Let's take a picture," Paulie says. "Then when we get back home we can prove what we found. I'll set my camera for time delay so we can both be in the shot."

You're quick to agree with Paulie's logic. As he sets his camera on a rock, and lines it up for the shot, you brush as much dirt and sand off it as you can.

Paulie hits a button on his phone then rushes over to where you've hoisted your end of the bone off the ground. Ten seconds later, both of you are straining under its weight and smiling like it's Christmas morning.

YOU SAY WHICH WAY

With a FLASH you're knocked off your feet.

As you brush the dust from your clothes you look around. "Have we jumped again?"

Paulie scans the canyon. "We must have, the creek is dry."

Then you see the big bone. "Did that come with us?"

"It must have."

"Wow, we should carry it back to camp."

"Carry it? We can barely pick it up," Paulie says, scrunching his forehead and looking at you like you're a moron.

You look at the bone and scratch your head. The bone has a slight curve to it. "I bet we could drag it like a sledge," you say. "We just need some rope or something."

You can see Paulie's mind working as he tries to solve the problem. Then he smiles. "If you don't mind sacrificing some clothing, we could twists some strips of fabric into cord and hook it onto our backpacks. Then we can drag the bone to camp."

"I've got a spare sweatshirt in my pack. That might work."

Paulie nods. "I've got one too. That should be plenty."

You set about cutting your sweatshirts into thin strips and braiding them into lengths of rope, then tie them together into an elongated Y. You attach the base of the Y to the bone and then tie the other two ends to your packs.

Like horses in harness, you and Paulie try out your contraption. With only a couple of feet of bone dragging on the ground like a big spoon, the going isn't too bad.

"Hey, I think this is going to work." You grin. "I knew there was a reason I brought you along. Now, mush!"

And you really are pleased. You don't know how you would have gone if you'd been out here alone. Even though Paulie is younger, having company has made a big difference to your confidence.

"There's only one problem," you say, remembering what you read in the guidebook. "Aren't we meant to mark the location of fossils we find and report it to the rangers so the park paleontologists can check out the site first?"

"But that law is recent," Paulie says with an evil grin. "We collected this fossil millions of years before that law was passed. Heck, we collected it before Montana even existed, and brought it back to the present. Technically, I reckon we're okay."

You give him a sideways glance. "Proving that might be tricky."

"Ah, but I've got the photos! They'll show water in the canyon."

"Sounds good enough to me," you say. "Assuming we've got the strength to get it back to camp."

Paulie looks pleased with himself. "We could sing a song to help us," he says. "Help us get a good rhythm going."

You look back at your prize and then over at Paulie. "Okay. Why not?"

And with that, Paulie breaks out into song. "Yo, heave ho, yo heave ho …"

66

By the time you're 100 yards from camp, a sea of amused faces stare at you. But this only makes you and Paulie sing louder.

"Well you two seem pleased with yourselves," Mister Jackson says as he comes out to greet you. "Looks like you've got quite a prize there. How did you come across that?"

You sneak a knowing look at Paulie and grin. "It's a long story Mister J. A very long and interesting story."

Congratulations, this part of your story is over. Well done. You've found a big dinosaur bone and have survived a trip back in time. What would you like to do now? Do you:

Go to the beginning and read a different path? **P1**

Or

Go to the list of choices and start reading from another part of the book? **P136**

Try to explain the time travel to Mister J.

The still-warm rock is in your right hand. Paulie's cell phone is in the other. "It wasn't fireworks, Mister J, it's this meteorite we found. It's causing us to jump back and forth in time."

"Funny. Ha, ha! Let me see that thing." Mister Jackson strides towards you with his arm outstretched.

You drop the rock into Mister Jackson's palm and wait for his reaction. "It certainly absorbs the heat from the sun. It's much warmer than I expected."

"It's been vibrating fast," Paulie says. "No wonder it's warm."

Your teacher ignores Paulie's comments and holds the rock up in front of his face, turning it from side to side. "Certainly looks like a meteorite. Where'd you find it?"

"Up near Gabriel's arch," you say. "We think it's reacting with Paulie's phone somehow. We got sent back to the Cretaceous era. There were dinosaurs and everything!"

"Yeah," Paulie says. "The climate changed too. The place was all swampy. We saw Troodons and a T. Rex!"

"Fossils?" Mister Jackson asks.

Paulie is hopping from foot to foot, getting more agitated by the minute. "No! Real ones! I swear Mister J. There were real dinosaurs!"

You nod your agreement, but the doubt in Mister J expression is obvious. "You should have seen them Mister J. They were awesome!"

"They tried to eat us!" Paulie says.

"Very funny," Mister Jackson says. He tosses the meteorite towards you. "Now go and catalogue your find and stop this nonsense." And with that, Mister J turns and heads back to the other parents sitting around the makeshift camp kitchen.

You turn to Paulie. "Well that went well. Still, it's no wonder he thinks we're nuts."

"Wouldn't you?" Paulie says. "I'm having problems believing what happened myself, and I was there!"

"So, what now?" you say. "Do we take Mister J on a time jump so he'll believe us?"

"I don't think that's a very good idea."

You turn towards the setting sun. The sky is streaked orange and red. "Let's sleep on it, Paulie. We can decide what to do in the morning."

Paulie agrees, just as one of the parents rings the dinner bell.

The next morning, despite being warm and comfortable in your sleeping bag, you get up early and throw a few chunks of wood onto the embers of last night's bonfire. The morning air is crisp and cool, but you know once the sun gets up the day will get quite warm.

As the new logs begin to pop and crackle, you grab a folding chair and sit, staring into the flames. It's hard to take your mind off the events of the previous day and you're pleased the others are still asleep. You need time to think.

The sun creeps over the ridge to the east and the first rays of light hit the tents. People begin to stir. The first adult up is Mister J. After making himself a cup of instant coffee, he pulls up a folding chair and sits beside you.

"So, what's all this dinosaur stuff about?" he says. "You and Paulie aren't usually ones to tell tall tales. What's got in to you two?"

"It's not a story, I swear Mister J. It really happened. I just wish I could figure out some way to prove it to you."

"So, this isn't some elaborate joke? You're actually serious?"

You nod. "We really did see dinosaurs Mister J. Honest we did."

Mister Jackson shakes his head in confusion. "Well, today the whole class is going up to the arch and beyond. Why don't you show me exactly where this time jump happened. Then we'll see if we can make sense of it. Maybe there's a logical explanation for what you two experienced."

"Thanks Mister J." At least he hasn't discounted your story out of hand. "You're right. There must be a logical explanation."

And with that Mister Jackson gets up and walks over to the camp kitchen. Then he turns. "You weren't eating cactus were you?"

You shake your head, wondering what he's on about. Mister J shrugs and heads off to help organize breakfast.

An hour later, all fed and watered, Mister Jackson, thirty students, and three of the six parents are ready to hike off into the hills. The group will retrace your path up to

Gabriel's arch and then move further into the canyon to a spot where fossils have been found before.

After packing your supplies for the day, you slot the meteorite into a side pocket of your daypack and walk towards Paulie's tent. His T. Rex flag hangs limp above its opening. "Don't forget your phone, Paulie," you say. "If we're going to reproduce the conditions for our time jump we'll need everything to be identical."

Paulie's head pop out. "Are you serious? You're actually considering going back in time again? Holy moly, you've got rocks in your head."

"Hey, this could be the biggest scientific breakthrough of the century. We could go down in history."

Paulie climbs out of his tent, dragging his pack behind him. "Or go down a T. Rex's throat. Don't you remember the close calls we had?"

"Yeah I know, but—"

Paulie hands you his cell phone. And then separately, its battery. "Here take it. Just tell me before you boot the thing up so I can get well away."

"But I thought you liked dinosaurs?"

"I like learning about them, not being eaten by them." He turns his back and wanders over to where the others are gathered.

You shrug, then slip the phone and battery into your pocket. At least Mister Jackson seems interested in getting to the bottom of this mystery.

"Okay everybody, listen up," Mister Jackson says. "The

first thing we're going to do is buddy up. Everyone find a buddy. At each stage of our fieldtrip, you have to make sure your buddy is with you before moving on. We don't want to leave anyone behind."

"Should we buddy up?" Mister Jackson says, looking down at you.

Paulie's wandered off and is standing next to one of his classmates so you say, "Sure, Mister J. Why not?"

"Right, let's go. We've got a fair distance to walk today so keep together, and keep an eye on your buddy."

Mister Jackson stops along the way and tells you about the history of the Badlands. It isn't until you get to the ridge where Gabriel's arch is located that the group stops for a break.

While you wait for your chance to talk to Mister Jackson, you look around the area, trying to remember where the T. Rex had been standing. By imagining yourself up on top of the arch, you walk along the ridge to a spot that look about the right distance from the arch. Here there is a patch of low scrubby bushes. While keeping an eye out for snakes, you scrabble around pulling the bushes aside, and looking for telltale signs of prehistoric life. It's then that you see the animal print in the rock.

When you see a second footprint your eyes widen. "Hey Mister J! Hey Paulie! Come and look at this!"

Mister Jackson, wanders over. "What's so urgent?"

You pull a branch aside. "Look."

Now you've got his attention.

"It's an old fossilized animal print of some sort," Mister J says. "Well spotted."

"It looks like the one we saw when we time jumped," Paulie says. "It's a Troodon print."

"You still sticking to that story?" Mister Jackson says as he studies the footprint in the sandstone more closely. "You probably saw this yesterday and decided to dream up this hoax."

You point to the second print. "Okay then how do you explain that!"

"These can't be that old, this looks like a boot print ... people weren't here…" But then he realizes the boot print is set in stone.

While Mister Jackson studies the print, you take off your boot. "Here, try this for fit."

Mister Jackson looks confused at first. And then he sees the chunk of heel that is missing from the sole of your boot and the corresponding shape in the rock. He grabs the shoe and places it into the impression made in the sandstone.

It fits perfectly.

"But how?"

"Exactly," you say kneeling down beside the footprint. "Unless Paulie and I were telling the truth."

"Give me another look at that meteorite," Mister Jackson says.

You open your pack and take out the shiny black rock and place it gently in Mister Jackson's hand. Then you pull out Paulie's cell phone, slip the battery into the slot in its back and replace the cover.

"So should I turn the phone on and see if we time jump Mister J?"

"No!" Paulie says, scrabbling away from you with a look of terror in his eyes.

Mister J glances at Paulie, then at you, and then back down at the rock. His hands are trembling.

"There's more danger than just dinosaurs, you know!" Paulie yells from ten yards away. "We could end up in the future too," he says. "What if we jump so far forward the earth is no longer habitable? We'll never get back."

You can see Mister Jackson's mind ticking over. Before you can stop him, the teacher stands up and, grunting with effort, throws the meteorite as far as he can.

As the rock flies over the edge of the cliff and sails down into the dense scrub below, you wonder for a moment what opportunities you've missed and what dangers you've been spared.

Then you turn to your teacher and look down at your finger hovering over the 'on' button on the Paulie's phone. "I guess that's a no then?"

"I think fossil hunting is exciting enough. Don't you?" Mister Jackson says with a look of relief in his eyes. "Besides, it probably wouldn't have worked a second time."

Now that the meteorite is gone, Paulie relaxes.

You shrug and give your teacher a smile "Yeah, you're probably right Mister J, you're probably right."

Or, maybe you'll come back when you're a few years

older and have a look for it.

Congratulations, this part of your story is over. It is time to make another decision. Do you:

Go back to the start and read a different track? **P1**

Or

Go to the list of choices and start reading from another part of the book? **P136**

Follow a dry watercourse to the canyon floor.

"Let's take the direct route," you say. "We'll end up in the top of the canyon that way."

Paulie peers down the slope. "It's pretty steep."

"We can always slide down on our butts if we have to."

With that, you inch your way over the edge, and with feet side-on to the hill, start slip-sliding your way down towards the canyon floor. Pebbles bounce past you as Paulie moves into the dry watercourse above you, adding loose stones to those already rolling like marbles underneath your feet.

A couple of times, you slip and fall on your backside, grazing your hand as you reach out for support, but for the most part progress is good.

Until you spot the rattlesnake.

With a sharp intake of breath, you dig in your heels and try to stop, but the pebbles under your feet have another idea. They roll off in front of you, bouncing down onto the snake, giving it a fright and causing it to coil up ready to strike.

"Snake!" you yell up to Paulie.

Rattle, rattle, rattle, rattle, rattle.

You're on your bottom now, doing your best to stop, but you're nearly upon the reptile. And it's not a small snake either!

Maybe you can kick it away?

The rattling is close now. The snake has a diamond shaped head and a thick body, bigger around than your arm.

Coiled up, it's hard to say how long it is, but it must be at least five feet.

You dig your fingers into the soil, but still you slide towards the rattling snake. It's too late. You're moving too fast.

Rattle, rattle, rattle, rattle, rattle! STRIKE!

A sharp stabbing pain runs up your leg.

"Owwww!" You kick out wildly, sending the snake slithering off down the hillside. "He got me!"

More pebbles clatter past you. Then Paulie stops beside you.

"Are you okay?

"I've just been bitten by a rattlesnake. What do you think?"

Lifting your knee towards your belly, you reach down and pull up the leg of your jeans. Half way between knee and ankle, are two puncture wounds. They are already red and inflamed.

"Okay keep calm," Paulie says. "I've read about snakebite and you're meant to keep quiet so you don't pump the poison around your system."

"I'm bleeding."

"Bleeding is good," Paulie says. "The blood will wash out some of the poison."

"Aren't you going to suck out the poison?"

Paulie shakes his head. "You've been watching too many old movies. That will just make me sick too. We'll let it bleed for a minute then wrap the wound up to keep it clean. Once we've done that I'll help you the rest of the way down. Then I'll run and get help."

As the blood seeps from the snakebite, a burning sensation surrounds the wound. "It hurts, Paulie."

"Don't be a baby," Paulie says as he rummages in his pack for something to put around your wound. "Did you know that over 8,000 people are bitten by poisonous snakes in North America each year. Guess how many die."

"2,000?"

"About eight," he says. "So stop worrying. You'll be okay."

You're not so sure. "Doesn't a big snake mean lots of poison?"

"What self respecting snake wants to waste all its poison up on you? You're not its lunch."

Paulie pulls a spare t-shirt out of his pack and starts ripping it into strips. He ties them loosely around your wound.

"Aren't you going to make a tourniquet?" you ask.

Paulie laughs. "No, that's from the movies too, silly. The poison from snake bites destroys tissue, it's better if it spreads a bit, it will be more diluted that way and cause less damage."

It's times like this you're pleased your companion is a nerd. "Just as well you know all this stuff. Remind me to recommend you for a medal when we get back."

Paulie gives you a smile as he finishes off a knot. "Okay, you're all bandaged up. Let's make a move. Just try to slide and not use your muscles any more than you have to. Lean on me."

You both make an awkward two-headed four-legged animal that half slides, half slips down the last of the hill to the canyon floor. Once there, Paulie props you up in the shade of a boulder.

"You're not supposed to eat or drink after being bitten by a rattlesnake. Just keep quiet and I'll be back as quickly as I can."

You look up at Paulie through vision that's going blurry. "Okay. Just hurry … and thanks."

"No prob."

Paulie jogs down the canyon towards camp. As his shape disappears around a corner, the throb in your leg increases. A burning sensation sears a path from the wound up into your thigh. You hope Paulie gets help in time.

You pull your pack over to use as a pillow. Now that the sound of Paulie's footsteps has gone, it's so quiet. All you can hear is the whistling wind as it comes up the canyon. Far above, a prairie falcon soars. You drift in and out of sleep. Then blackness takes you.

You're not sure how long you've been out, when you hear someone calling your name. It sounds like Paulie. Lifting yourself up on one elbow, you peer down the canyon. A number of blurry shapes appear. It's hard to see who they are, but at least someone is coming. Exhausted, you flop back down. Never before has your body ached so much. Then, as you're about to drift off again, hands lift you onto a stretcher.

"Hang on there, we've got you now," a man's voice you don't recognize says.

There is a sharp prick in your arm.

"That should make you feel better."

When you wake up, you're in a room with white walls. It smells of disinfectant and it's dark outside. Near the window, Paulie is asleep in a chair and the ward is reasonably quiet apart from the squeak of rubber shoes on hospital linoleum and the *beep, beep, beep* of a monitor somewhere.

Paulie is still wearing the same clothes but he's washed his face. You cough, and reach for a glass of water on the cabinet beside you.

"Oh you're awake," Paulie says, rubbing his eyes. "How do you feel?"

"I've been better, but I'm alive, thanks to you."

"You really scared me," Paulie says.

"I thought you said I'd be fine. That not many people died of snakebite."

"Yeah, well I didn't want to worry you. On the bright side, Doc says you'll be okay to leave tomorrow afternoon. You'll just have to take it easy for a few days."

"No more fossil hunting, eh?" you say, giving your friend a smile.

"Not this year. But there is some good news. They caught those fossil smugglers. I forgot all about them when you tangled with that rattler. But it seems you were talking in your sleep and one of the paramedics asked me if what you were saying was true or just a nightmare. I said it was true and told them about the men. They got on the radio and contacted the police."

"Wow, that's great," you say, resting your head back down on your pillow.

"It's been exciting alright. I got to give a statement to one of the policemen. Did you know that police capture over three thousand…"

You drift off to the sound of Paulie telling you all the facts he's learned about the police. It's quite comforting, almost like having someone read you a story.

This part of your story is over. But have you tried all the different paths? Have you found fossils? Have you found gold? Have you been hunted by the T. Rex?

It is time to make a decision. Do you:

Go to the beginning and read a different track? **P1**

Or

Go to the list of choices and start reading somewhere else in the book? **P136**

You have decided to keep the secret to yourself.

You pull Paulie aside. "Let's keep this to ourselves. They'll think we've gone crazy if we try to explain."

Paulie nods. "I'm still trying to convince myself it actually happened. Have you heard of mass hallucinations? Maybe we had one of those."

"I don't think that foul-breathed T. Rex was a hallucination." You pluck at your sleeve and take a sniff. "I can still smell his slobber on my clothes."

Paulie lifts the hem of his t-shirt and buries his nose in the fabric. "Yep, that's T. Rex all right."

"Besides, we may want to go back again," you say. "If we tell Mister J, he'll just stop us."

Paulie's eyes widen. "Are you serious? You want to go back?" He shakes his head slowly from side to side and whistles through his teeth. "Holy moly! You're nutzo!"

"But, what an opportunity. I thought you liked dinosaurs."

"I do," Paulie says." I like them in books and movies and museums where they belong."

"But to see really see them.... Where's your sense of adventure?"

"Where's *your* sense of self preservation? In case you've forgotten, we nearly got eaten back there. What happens if we end up right in the middle of them with nowhere to run? What then?"

Paulie does have a point.

"Well, let's sleep on it and decide in the morning. We just need to think of a safe place to time-jump from. Somewhere the dinosaurs won't be able to get at us. Please, think about it, Paulie. We could make history!"

Paulie scratches his head. "Okay I'll think on it. But no guarantees."

You're about to tell Paulie about the possibility of winning a Nobel Prize when the dinner bell rings and the camp erupts with screaming kids running towards the picnic tables.

After eating hotdogs and salad, your group sits around the campfire, singing songs and roasting marshmallows. Paulie avoids eye contact with you, so you give him time to think. Push too hard and he'll turn you down for sure.

Then, as a nearly full moon rises over the hills in the distance, Mister Jackson yawns loudly and stands up. "Okay everyone, time to hit the sack. We've got a busy day tomorrow."

The next morning you're one of the first up. Last night, it had taken you a while to get to sleep, and when you did, you'd dreamed of standing on Gabriel's arch looking at a T. Rex. In your dream, the massive dinosaur had ignored the Troodons and walked right up to you. And even though you were standing atop your rocky perch, its massive head was level with yours. The beast's teeth were long and sharp, and as it tilted its head sideways, one of its eyes, big as a softball, stared directly at you, its pupil black and glistening. You remember your frightened face reflecting back from the eyeball's shiny surface. Then, when you turned to find Paulie, he was nowhere to be seen.

The dream had been so real you'd startled yourself awake and then spent the next half hour staring at the nylon roof of your tent with every nerve in your body tingling. Even after the tremors had stopped, sleep would not return. Finally, after dawn's weak light penetrated the walls of your tent, you'd given up, climbed out of your sleeping bag, and gone outside to prod the campfire awake.

As you stir the embers and add small pieces of wood to them, you think about going back in time again. It's a scary idea, but despite the bad dream, the concept is frightening in an exciting way. This could be the defining moment of your life. The one time that sets you apart from the crowd. Your one chance to become an internet sensation. You could start a science channel online, or write a book about your experiences. Or both!

Then you remember Paulie's words. He's right, the dinosaurs would eat you without a moment's hesitation. But is it worth the risk?

You're deep in thought when Paulie sits down beside you.

"How'd you sleep?" he asks.

"Not very good," you reply. "You?"

Paulie's yawns then looks up with bleary eyes. "I kept thinking about that T. Rex. It's a wonder anything survived with those things around."

"Yeah but—"

Paulie holds his hand up to stop you. "Look, I've decided.

I'm not going back, but I won't stop you if you want to go."
Paulie hands you his phone, and then its battery, which he's
taken out. "Just give me enough time to stand clear if you
decide to go for it. Okay?"

"But Paulie, I thought we were a team."

Paulie shakes his head. "No we're—"

"We are, Paulie! We're the only ones who have ever gone
back in time. Do you know what that means?"

Paulie glares at you. "It means we're lucky to be alive."

"No, it means we've got a chance to make a difference.
We can go back and take photographs so that scientists
know exactly what these animals looked like. Remember the
feathers we saw on the Troodons? Aren't the experts are still
arguing about that sort of thing?"

Not being drawn in, Paulie closes his eyes. His hands fly
up to cover his ears. He shakes his head and mumbles "No,
no, no, no," under his breath.

You pull down one of his arms. "Come on, Paulie, please!
You know you want to."

He stops rocking and looks up at you. "You should tell
Mister Jackson what happened to us." Then he stands up
and walks away.

You look down at the phone and the battery, then
towards Paulie as he nears his tent.

It is time to make a decision. Do you:

Have a go at time jumping on your own? **P85**

Or

Tell Mister Jackson what happened? **P88**

You have decided to time jump on your own.

"Okay, I'll do it myself!" you yell at Paulie's back.

After slotting the battery back into Paulie's phone, you take the meteorite and hold it out in your hand. You hold the phone over the rock and push the power button and wait.

"Who are you yelling at?" Mister Jackson says.

"Nobody Mister J." You inhale deeply trying to steady your nerves as you wait for the phone to power up. Then as the phone's screen turns on, the meteorite begins to glow. You can feel its vibrations pulsing through your arm.

"And what's that?"

"Nothing Mister J."

"Doesn't look like nothing to me," your teacher says, glaring at the rock in your hand. "What are you playing at?"

"I'd move back if I were you, Mister J." You stand up and take a few steps away from your teacher. "Watch out! This thing's about to go off!"

"What the–"

FLASH.

Mister Jackson is staring at you and waving the smoke away from his face. "What the heck was that?" Then he looks around at the steaming jungle.

You give your teacher a sheepish smile. "Welcome to the late Cretaceous, Mister J."

Mister Jackson's face is a mask of confusion. "Don't be ridiculous!" he says. "Time travel is imposs–"

The roar of the T. Rex is unmistakable. You and Mister Jackson spin around towards the sound. The beast is running towards you. It has two friends with it this time.

"My God! What have you done?"

Mister Jackson sprints off into the dense ferns, running for his life. You're about to take off after him, when your alarm buzzes and you spring upright in bed. Sweat drips off your forehead. Despite being in a familiar place you look around for signs of dinosaurs before realizing it's all a dream and today is the day you leave on your field trip to the Badlands of Montana to look for dinosaur fossils.

"Phew," you mumble as you swing your legs off the bed and start thinking about getting dressed for the field trip. "That was a little too real."

Quite a few hours later, on a bus in Montana, a meteorite streaks across a cloudless sky and disappears behind a hill not far away.

"Wow did you see that?" Paulie says, as he points towards the horizon.

A couple of students look up from their phones. "What? Huh?"

Paulie waves his hand excitedly. "The meteorite! Over there! Did you see it?"

"Yeah I saw it, Paulie," you say, remembering you dream. "But if you happen to stumble across it while out fossil hunting all I can say is leave it alone."

"What? Why?" he says giving you a strange look. "Are

you okay?"

You shrug and give him a smile. "Do you believe in premonitions?"

Paulie shakes his head. "No. Don't be silly."

"What about time travel?" you ask.

Paulie smiles back. "Well now that's a different story. Did you know that Albert…"

You turn and look out the window, ignoring Paulie as he rambles on about the space-time continuum and Einstein's special theory of relativity. You admire the rugged beauty of the Badlands and wonder what adventures the next few days will bring. Whatever happens, there's one thing you do know for sure. You won't be picking up any meteorites this trip. Especially with all the cell phones around.

You have reached the end of this part of the story, but you still have decisions to make. Do you:

Go back to the start and read a different track? **P1**

Or

Go to the list of choices and start reading from another part of the story? **P136**

You have decided to tell Mister Jackson what happened.

Maybe Paulie is right. There are so many dangers involved with going back in time. Who knows which era you'd jump to if you went back a second time. And where would you land? Amongst a pack of Velociraptors? Without understanding how these jumps are happening and how to control things, there is just too much that could go wrong.

It would take a proper expedition, fitted out with modern equipment and some form of protection to have any chance of survival in such a hostile environment for any length of time. Unlike modern times, where humans are at the top of the food chain, during the age of the dinosaur, they were the top predators.

Having made your decision, you take the meteorite and Paulie's cell phone and go looking for Mister Jackson. When you find him, he's leaning against an old stone wall, drinking coffee at the camp kitchen with a couple of the other parents. You are so concerned about what you're going to say to him, you don't notice he is sending a text.

Startled, you jump back and look down at the meteorite expecting it to turn red at any moment. But nothing's happening. How can that be? Why would Paulie's phone make the meteorite send you back and forth in time, while Mister Jackson's doesn't? It just doesn't make sense. Is there some weird fault in Paulie's phone that is reacting with the meteorite?

"What's up with you?" Mister Jackson says. "You look

like you've seen a ghost."

Again, you look at his phone and then at the rock in your hand. "I'm trying to understand—"

"Understand what?" Mister Jackson says, sliding his phone into his pocket and taking a step towards you. "Why are you acting so strange? And what's that in your hand?"

"It's a meteorite Paulie and I found when we went walking yesterday afternoon." You hold the rock up for Mister Jackson to see. "But it's got some strange properties we can't understand."

"Properties?" Mister Jackson asks. "What's that supposed to mean?"

"It's hard to explain, Mister J."

The teacher grabs your sleeve and leads you over to a couple folding chairs, away from the others. You and Mister Jackson sit face to face.

"Okay, tell me. What's going on?"

"It's hard to know where to start," you say.

Mister Jackson's eyes bore into you. "How about at the beginning. That usually works."

You watch his expression as you tell your story – about picking up the meteorite, standing under the arch, the T. Rex, the Troodons. Everything. By the time you reach the end, Mister Jackson is left with his mouth slightly ajar and a confused look on his face.

"Do you seriously expect me to believe that?" he says.

You shake your head. "No, I can barely believe it myself … but it's true."

"Give me the meteorite and Paulie's phone," Mister Jackson says, holding out his hand.

You do as you're told.

"So this happened when you took a picture, and again when the phone booted up?"

You nod and feel yourself blush. Why you're embarrassed about telling the truth you're not quite sure. Maybe it's because the story sounds so far-fetched.

Without another word, Mister Jackson slots the battery into Paulie's phone. He holds his finger over the on button. "So you're saying if I turn this phone on I'm going to jump back in time?"

You stand up and take a few steps back. "I'd be careful if I were you Mister J. I swear I'm telling you the truth."

"Ha!" he scoffs. "What do you take me for? You kids and your silly stories." He pushes the button.

"Mister J!" You jump back a couple of steps back and stare at the meteorite. At first nothing happens, but then as the phone goes through its start-up sequence, the rock starts to glow.

"Look," you say. The rock glows brighter and brighter. "It's happening!"

Mister Jackson stares at the rock. His eyes widen. Then with a flash Mister Jackson disappears into thin air.

"Whoa!" You look around to see if anyone else saw what happened. But instead of gasping in shock at the disappearance of their teacher, the students are pouring cereal into bowls and toasting bread over the campfire, oblivious to what's just happened.

Now what do you do? You stand there looking at the spot where Mister Jackson used to be. You can still see his boot prints in the dirt. Hopefully, an idea will pop into your head.

You look up and see Paulie's T. Rex flag fluttering over his tent. Who else would believe what just happened? You race over and pull back the flap. "Hey, Paulie. You're not going to believe what just happened," you say, crawling in. "Mister J didn't believe me when I told him about going back in time and he turned on your phone. Now he's vanished!"

"Vanished?"

"Gone back in time! I tried to warn him."

Paulie cradles his head with both hands and closes his eyes. He rocks slowly back and forth mumbling under his breath.

"Don't zone out on me, Paulie. What are we going to do?"

His head snaps up and his eyes squint at you. "What can we do? Nothing. That's what."

"But surely we should tell someone."

Paulie laughs. "Like they're really going to believe us. They're more likely to think we've gone crazy, killed our teacher and buried him somewhere out in the desert."

"You've been watching too much T.V. Why would they think that?" you say. "We're just a couple of kids. I'm going to go tell one of the parents. Come on Paulie. Back me up.

Surely they'll believe both of us."

Paulie sighs. You can sense his reluctance. "I don't know…"

"Paulie, come on, we have to tell someone!"

For a moment he sits in silence. A last he does a little shake, like a chill has run down his back and then, on hands and knees, makes a move towards the entrances of the tent. "All right. Let's get it over with."

Once out of the tent, you start walking towards a group of parents. Suddenly there is a FLASH and a puff of smoke off to your left. Then, from behind a clump of sagebrush, his shirt in tatters, soot smudges on his face and gasping like he's been running, Mister Jackson appears.

You and Paulie rush over to him. "You okay, Mister J?"

His hand shakes as you take the phone from it and remove the battery. The meteorite is in his other hand so you take it and drop it into your pocket. Your teacher barely notices. Instead, he stares straight ahead, like a statue.

With the phone and meteorite tucked safely away, you grab Mister Jackson's arm and give it a shake. "Mister J? Can you hear me? Mister J?"

"He's in shock," Paulie says.

"A … Daspletosaurus … nearly … got … me." Mister Jackson says, a bubble of drool running down his lower lip.

You and Paulie lead Mister Jackson over to a seat by the fire where he sits trembling for a few minutes before turning to you.

The teacher wipes his mouth with his sleeve. "Sorry … I

… didn't … believe–"

"Holy moly, Mister Jackson," Paulie says. "Sounds like you had a narrow escape."

Mister Jackson slowly moves his head up and down a few times, then slaps his cheeks lightly with his hands. A rush of air escapes his lungs and he looks over at Paulie. "It was … awful. Incredible, but awful at the same time. I can't believe…"

"Where did you end up?" Paulie asks.

"I'm not exactly sure. But as I was wandering around the jungle trying to figure out how to get back, I came upon a group of Daspletosaurs ripping some poor creature to bits."

"Must have been late Cretaceous then," Paulie says. "That's where we went too."

"Yeah, well one of the critters saw me and I had to run for it. Kept getting hooked up on branches as I ran through the jungle. I hid behind a tree and turned off the phone and then rebooted it. The thing took ages to get going again. I was nearly lunch."

"I did warn you Mister J," you say. "But I'm glad you made it back in one piece. We were just trying to work out how to break the bad news of your disappearance to the others when you reappeared."

"So what now?" Paulie asks. "Do we tell the others?"

"Or do we keep it secret," you suggest. "We could come back over summer and do some real exploring. What do you say Mister J, should we organize a proper expedition and come back? We'd be famous. Imagine all the exciting things we could discover."

"We should take the phone and meteorite to the Smithsonian, or some research institution," Mister Jackson says. "I certainly don't want you children getting in harm's way." He pats his pockets. "Where is the phone?"

You stab Paulie a look, then turn back to Mister Jackson. "Didn't you bring it back with you?" Your right hand moves over the lump of rock in your pocket, shielding it from Mister Jackson's view.

Confused, Mister Jackson searches his pockets. He finds nothing but a set of keys and a penknife. "I–I must have dropped it somewhere. He looks at the ground around his feet, then walks back around the sagebrush. "It's gone. What a shame."

Paulie scowls at you, but you raise a finger to your lips and signal him to remain silent.

"Well I'm going to go write my experience down in my notebook while everything is still fresh in my mind. You two should do the same. We still might be able to provide some information scientists can use, however vague it may be."

"Good idea Mister J," you say, dragging Paulie by the sleeve towards the tents.

"But I saw you take the phone and meteorite out of his hand," Paulie whispers. "Why are you lying?"

"I'm not lying. I'm protecting our discovery, Paulie. This is a once in a lifetime chance to–"

Paulie is looking over your shoulder. You stop talking and turn around. It's Mister Jackson. He's standing there with is hand held out.

"What?" you ask.

"Hand them over. Just as well my memory came back. Knowing you two, you'd probably rush off and get yourself killed."

"But Mister J," you say. "We're the ones who found–"

"Give them up," Paulie says. "Mister Jackson is right. It's too dangerous."

You shrug and dig the phone and meteorite out of your pockets. "No one is going to believe us, you know. They'll think we've gone crazy when you tell them what happened."

"Under normal circumstances I'd agree with you. Except that I took photos while I was back in time." In his excitement to show you his pictures, and still suffering from shock, Mister Jackson slots the battery into the phone and hits the on button. "Here have a look."

Before you have a chance to jump back, the meteorite glows red and there is a FLASH.

Suddenly it is hot and sticky and thick ferns and forest surround you. Strange flying reptiles soar overhead.

"Holy moly, Mister J!" Paulie yells. "Look at what you've done!"

"Wow," you say. "Look over there, Pachycephalosaurs. They're butting heads."

The two animals are crashing through the jungle and slamming their horned heads together in some strange duel. Their screams are ear splitting as they rush towards each other.

Unfortunately, not one of you hear the two T. Rex's sneaking up behind you.

The T. Rex's look at each other and drool, as if to say "lunch is served."

You've reached the end of this part of the story. But have you tried all the different paths? It is time to make another decision. What would you like to do now?

Start the story over and try a different path? **P1**

Or

Go to the list of choices and start reading from another part of the story? **P136**

You have decided to go further into the mine.

"There could be tons of rock, Paulie. Digging ourselves out could take hours … or days." You turn and shine your light further into the mine. Then you lick your finger and hold it up.

Paulie gives you a strange look. "What are you doing?"

"Testing for wind. It's faint, but I can still feel it. Come on, let's get moving before the flashlight runs out."

Paulie grins. "You sure you didn't fart?" he says, trying to make light of the situation.

You laugh. "Well if I did, even more reason to keep moving."

As you head deeper into the mine, there are many side shafts. Most only go back ten or fifteen yards before coming to a dead end. One of them holds a pile of old cable, lengths of chain and other rusty equipment.

The temperature gets colder as you descend deeper and deeper. You take a sweatshirt out of your pack and slip it on.

"This isn't looking very ho–hopeful," Paulie says nervously, pulling a sweater out of his pack. "How will we know which way leads to the surface?"

"Be quiet for a moment," you say. Then you lick your finger once more. As you stand quietly feeling for breeze you hear the faint trickle of water off in the distance.

Paulie cups a hand around one ear. "You hear that?"

"Come on, I can still feel a breeze, let's find out where it's coming from."

With more urgency, you and Paulie push forward. About five minutes later the floor of the tunnel starts showing signs of moisture. There are puddles on the floor, and rivulets running down the rock walls of the mine.

Then suddenly, the beam of your flashlight disappears into nothingness.

Throwing your arm out, you yell, "Stop!"

The ground in front of you is gone. When you shine the flashlight at your feet, you're standing near the edge of a vertical drop. How far down it goes is anyones guess. But one thing for sure is that the breeze is blowing harder here.

Inching forward you shine the light into the void. "It's a huge cavern!"

"I've read about these," Paulie says. "Ground water eats away at the softer rock, and over thousands of years it leaves a cave system behind."

"Do you think there's a stream down there?"

"Makes sense," Paulie says. "The water has to go somewhere."

"Maybe it leads to the outside?"

He nods. "It's possible. But how do we get to it?"

On hands and knees you crawl to the edge and peer over. The beam from the flashlight is quite dim by the time it hits the water. "It's a stream alright," you say. "It's not that far, twenty-five feet or so."

"How deep is the water?"

"I can't tell," you say rising from your knees.

Paulie is shivering. "So what now?" he asks.

Then you remember the rusty cable you saw in one of the side tunnels. "Let's get some cable and climb down. We can follow the stream out of the mine."

"How long can you tread water?" Paulie asks.

"How long can you go without food and water?" you reply.

After dragging a length of cable back through the tunnel, you tie one end around one of the heavy support timbers and then drag the remainder to the edge of the drop off and toss it over the side. There is a satisfying splash from below as the cable hits the water.

"This isn't going to be easy to hang on to," Paulie says, looking at the cable. "It's going to be rough on our hands."

He's right. The cable isn't that big around either. It will be hard to hang on to something so skinny.

As you stand there trying to come up with a solution, Paulie reaches down and unbuckles one of the shoulder straps of his daypack. He wraps the strap around his hands and then grabs onto the cable and gives it a tug.

"I think this might work," he says. "It's not as good as a glove, but it's better than nothing."

"Okay," you say. "I'll give you some light while you climb down. Then I'll toss down our packs and climb down myself."

Paulie hands you the other strap from his pack and then gets on his hands and knees and slowly maneuvers his way back to the edge. With a grasp on the cable he lowers his legs over and then the rest of his body.

"Whooooah! I'm slipppppppppping!" he yells.

SPLASH!

You lean over the edge and sweep the beam of your flashlight back and forth. Then you see Paulie's head poking out of the water, his hand hanging onto the cable.

"You okay?"

"Yeah fine," he yells up. "The water's really deep and there's a current."

"Okay, well hold on to the cable. Here come the packs."

"Toss me the light too," Paulie say. "I'll light your way as you climb down."

When you drop the flashlight, you are cast into darkness. You wrap the strap of Paulie's pack around your hands and grip the cable, lowering yourself over the edge just as Paulie did. With your feet pressed against the wall of the cave you manage to half abseil, half slide down the cable.

"Brrrrr… Why didn't you tell me the water was so cold?"

"Yeah well, there wasn't anything I could do about that, so there wasn't any point."

Your pull as much of your body as possible out of the water and up onto your floating backpack. Thankfully, all the air trapped inside makes it quite buoyant. "At least we can float downstream," you say. "Give me the light back. I'll lead the way."

So, with your head and shoulders out of the water, and kicking with your feet, you and Paulie head off into the unknown. You make good progress, but it doesn't take long for the chill from the water to seep into your bones. After fifteen minutes, your toes are numb.

Then, just as you're about to think you've made a terrible mistake, a pinpoint of light appears in the distance. "Paulie! Do you see it?" You turn the flashlight back onto Paulie and see him, grimly hanging on to his pack, his teeth chattering, lips turning blue. "Hang on. It's not far now."

When you finally pop out from under a rock ledge and into a shimmering pool, relief floods through your body. Never did you think that seeing the sky would give you such joy.

The pool is about ten yards wide and surrounded on three sides by smooth rock that rises up to create a natural bowl. The fourth side is open and the water from the pool trickles down a narrow watercourse.

Shivering, you and Paulie drag yourselves out of the water and flop down like seals basking in the sun.

The warm rock is the best thing you've ever felt, and before long, you can feel your toes again. Even the chattering of Paulie's teeth has stopped.

"You ready to head back to camp, Paulie?"

He rolls over, leaving a wet print of his body on the sandstone. "Let me toast the other side first."

You roll over onto your back and close your eyes. "Fine with me. It's no fun walking with wet clothes anyway."

Within twenty minutes, the sun has dried your clothes and warmed you through. You stand up and look down the watercourse. "I wonder where we are. Do you think this stream will lead us back towards camp?"

Paulie looks up at the position of the sun. "It should do. The sun is setting behind us. East is towards camp so…"

While Paulie reattaches the straps to his pack, you climb up the slope behind the pool to see if you can get your bearings. As you crest the ridge, you see a pickup truck parked behind a couple of boulders off to the north. The truck has chunky fat tires suitable for the sandy terrain. In the tray are what look like bones. Huge bones.

You squat down in case the smugglers are about and study the area. The truck has come along a rough track from the main road. They've parked as close as they can get to their stockpile of bones in the abandoned mine.

The camp is off in the distance. Paulie was right about the watercourse heading the right way.

You watch for a few minutes. There is no sign of the men, so you slide back down to Paulie. "I can see the smuggler's truck," you tell him. "It's just over the ridge, hidden from view."

"Any sign of them?" he asks.

You shake your head. "No, but we'll have to cross their path between the mine and the truck to get to camp."

Paulie looks worried. "We can't let them know we've escaped. They'll hightail it out of here before we can alert the authorities."

Then you have an idea. "Do you know how to hotwire a truck, Paulie?"

He starts shaking his head. "No … and even if I could, I don't steal."

"Even from smugglers?"

"It's still theft." Paulie unzips the side pocket of his pack and pulls out his cell phone. He wipes the phone on his shirt. "It's still working, but there's no signal."

"Well, if we can't phone the authorities, and you don't want to take their truck, maybe we could disable it somehow?"

"Like let the air out of their tires?"

You smile. "That would do the trick."

"But what if they catch us? Wouldn't it be better to get to camp and phone the police?"

Calling the police makes sense, but what if the smugglers take the dinosaur bones and leave before the police arrive?

It is time to make a decision. What should you do? Do you:

Try to disable the smuggler's truck? **P110**

Or

Rush back to camp? **P120**

You have decided to dig your way out.

"I think we should dig ourselves out," you say. "Hold the light while I dig. When I get tired, you can have a turn."

Paulie swallows hard and nods. "Okay, but hurry."

After five minutes, you realize the hopelessness of your task. The light is already starting to fade and you've made very little progress.

"Come on, Paulie, there's no way we're going to get through this lot." You throw down the pick in frustration and snatch the flashlight out of Paulie's hand. "Let's find that other exit."

Another couple of hundred yards into the hillside, the tunnel splits in two. Down one tunnel, water is running, so you take the other. The breeze feels stronger here.

There is a slight vibration in the rock beneath your feet. You stop and listen for a moment. You turn back to Paulie. "Can you hear that?"

Paulie cups his ear. "Sounds like a generator."

"What? Down here?"

Paulie nods. "My uncle has a generator up at his cabin that sounds like that..."

The two of you pick up your pace. Further along the tunnel, the putt, putt, putting of generator becomes louder.

"I smell fumes," Paulie says.

"That's not a good sign. We'll die of carbon monoxide poisoning if they get too strong."

Fifty yards further on, you come to another split in the

passage. A large electrical cable runs up one tunnel and into the other. This time you take the one that goes away from the noise of the generator. Already you are beginning to cough. You need to get away from the fumes.

Three minutes down this side tunnel you both stop, not quite believing what you see.

"What is a door doing way down here?" Paulie asks.

"I don't know, but I hope it's not locked."

Paulie looks confused. "And why do they need electricity?"

The door is made of steel. It fits snugly into a rectangular hole cut into the side of the shaft. The cable runs through a conduit drilled into the rock beside the door. You reach for the handle and push down on the lever. The door swings open.

Neon lights flicker, then switch on. The room is full of stainless steel benches and laboratory equipment. On the far side of the lab is another door.

Paulie walks around inspecting the equipment. "This is a centrifuge," he says pointing a piece of equipment, the size of a microwave, sitting on one of the benches. "And this is a gel box. I've read about this stuff. It's used for extracting DNA."

"But why would anyone want—" Then you see the dinosaur bone on another table. It's been sliced down the center and the marrow has been scraped out and put into test tubes sitting in a rack beside it. "Paulie!"

"Wow," he says. "Someone's trying to clone dinosaurs!"

"Very clever," says the man in a lab coat as he comes through the door, carrying a big bottle of isopropyl alcohol "That's exactly what I'm doing."

"But why are you doing it down here?" Paulie asks.

The man laughs and sets the bottle on a bench. "Come, I'll show you." He walks back to the door and pulls it open. "Follow me."

You have second thoughts about going with the man, but he seems friendly and his story makes sense. Besides, it's not like you've got much choice if you're going to get out of here.

Through the door is a long corridor with doors running off it every ten yards or so. Each door has a glass panel in it, and when you look though them you see more people working on different projects.

"What is this place?" you ask.

"Well, as you probably guessed, it's a lab. It used to be a missile silo, but when it was decommissioned, the University of Montana took it over as a research centre."

"So you're not connected to those men who tried to kill us?" you ask.

"Kill you?" The man looks genuinely confused. "Which men?"

You and Paulie explain how you came to be in the mine. How the men collapsed the shaft, and how you found the door.

"And you say these men have a big pile of dinosaur bones?"

"Yes," you and Paulie say in unison.

"Well that's great news," the man says suddenly excited. "We're in need of some more bones. So far we've not been able to isolate any DNA. Too old, unfortunately. But if what you say is true, the pile those men have collected should give us a chance to find some."

"So you're going to bring the dinosaurs back?" asks Paulie.

"I know, you're thinking Jurassic Park. But no, we don't want that. We do, however, want to discover more about these creatures, and how they evolved."

You point to a phone hanging on the wall. "Well you'd better call the cops and get them to stop those men from getting away. Otherwise you'll be out of luck."

"Yes. And then, we'd better get you back to your school group," the man says. "They must be worried. Maybe you'd like to bring them back tomorrow for a tour of our facility?"

Paulie's eyes go wide. "Could we? That would be fantastic! Did you know that T. Rex was–"

"Hang on, Paulie," you say. "You can discuss all this tomorrow."

"Yes," the man says. "Tomorrow we'll have plenty of time to talk. Right now, I've got a call to make about those smugglers."

After his phone call, the man takes you along another corridor to a foyer with two elevators in it. The ride is quick. Once you're back on the surface, you see how well the complex is hidden from view. The only part visible is a concrete building covered in the local rock. It houses the machinery for the elevator. Outside, half a dozen cars sit in a dusty lot next to the park headquarters, a mile or so from the campground entrance on the main road.

"That's my blue pickup," the man says. "Jump in. I'll give you a ride back to your camp."

Mister Jackson stops what he's doing and looks up as the pickup pulls into the campground. "So what trouble did you two get into?" Mister Jackson asks as you get out of the Ford. "I hope you haven't embarrassed the school."

The man from the lab chuckles. "No, nothing like that. In fact, these two have been quite helpful." Then he explains the situation and repeats his invitation for the students to tour the dinosaur lab. "See you tomorrow at ten," the man says, getting back into his truck.

You and Paulie wave as he drives away.

Once the pickup is gone, Mister Jackson puts his hands on his hips and stares down at you. "Well it sounds like you two had quite an adventure."

Paulie is so excited about the lab visit, he can hardly contain himself. "Did you know that the lab used to be a missile silo and that there's all sorts of equipment they're using to extract DNA…"

You look at Mister Jackson. He raises an eyebrow and nods towards Paulie. Paulie hasn't noticed that the two of you have stopped listening. He's still rambling on about the lab.

When Mister Jackson starts laughing, you join in, unable

to help yourself.

Paulie stops talking, looks first to you and then to your teacher. He seems confused. "Wha–what's going on? Did I say something funny?"

Congratulations, this part of your story is over. You have done well, escaped from the smugglers and discovered the hidden lab. Now you get to tour the facilities with your classmates. But have you tried the other paths?

Now it's time to make another decision. Do you:

Go back to the beginning and read a different track? **P1**

Or

Go to the list of choices and choose a different place to start reading? **P136**

110

You have decided to try to disable the truck.

"I think we should sneak down to the truck and let their tires down," you say. "You don't want them to escape, do you?"

"No, but—"

"But what?"

"But we're just kids. And—and those guys have a gun."

You'd forgotten about the pistol. Maybe this isn't such a good idea after all. Then you have an idea. If you get Paulie to keep an eye out for the smugglers, he can warn you if they return. What other option is there?

"Come with me, Paulie." You lead him up the slope to where you first saw the truck. Off to the right is the track that leads up to the mine. To your left is the truck.

"See over there," you say pointing. "The smugglers will have to come along that track to get to where they've parked. You just need to sit up here and signal if you see them coming."

Paulie looks unsure. "How will I do that?"

From the depths of your pack, you pull out a bright orange t-shirt. "Here, wave this."

"Are you sure?"

You nod. "We can't let the bad guys get away, can we?"

"Okay, but be careful," Paulie says.

You take the pocketknife out of your pack. Then you grab your water bottle. You leave your pack behind in case you have to run for it.

"Back soon," you say.

The climb down to where the truck is parked takes you longer than expected. It's too steep to go in a straight line, especially with all the erosion and wash outs. Instead, you follow a ridge that runs off to the east for a quarter of a mile or so, before angling back.

About half way down the hill, you look back. Paulie is crouched on the ridge, the balled up t-shirt in his hand.

So far so good.

When you reach the truck, it is bigger than expected. It sits high off the ground on huge knobby tires. A spare is mounted on a steel rack over the cab in between a pair of spotlights. You'll need to deflate at least two tires to slow these guys down.

The small black cap over the air valve of the first tire comes off easily. You find a stick and use it to depress the metal pin on the valve. A hiss of air escapes. But a couple of minutes later, the tire is barely down. This is going to take ages.

You glance up at Paulie and feel your stomach lurch. He's on his feet waving the t-shirt frantically. Your heart races. "Rats! Time for plan B."

You put out your knife and open the longest blade. The blade looks tiny against the truck's big off-road tires. Still, it's your only hope. You stab the side of the tire a couple times. The sudden hiss of air sounds like an angry cobra as it escapes through the punctures. You move to the front of the vehicle and stab the left front tire too.

With the sabotage done, you run back towards the ridge keeping low and using what little scrub there is as cover.

You watch out for the men as you climb. Then, after gaining a bit of altitude, you see them. Both are carrying dinosaur bones over their shoulder. Thankfully, they are watching the ground as they walk, keeping an eye out for rattlers, perhaps. You sidle around the ridge, putting some rock between you and the men. No point in taking any chance of being spotted.

It's tougher climbing along the side of the ridge, and you have to watch your footing. But at least you're out of the men's sight.

By the time you reach Paulie, he is lying on his stomach, peering over the ridge, watching the men's progress. "They're nearly at the truck," he says.

You crouch down to watch. As they near the truck, one of them throws his bone on the ground and starts yelling. His curses float up on the breeze.

"He's not a happy camper," you say with a smirk.

"Aw… poor little smuggler."

The man is kicking the truck's tires, yelling and screaming at his companion who is looking around, trying to see who has done this. His face turns towards the ridge.

"Get down!" Paulie says, grabbing your arm and jerking you off balance.

You land flat on the ground. "Hey!"

"Sorry, but I think he saw you," Paulie says. "Let's get out of here."

"Yep. We need to make it to camp before they do. Otherwise who knows what they'll do."

With that, you skid back down to the pool, skirt around its cool water and head downstream. "Watch your footing, Paulie, some of these rocks are slippery."

The creek doesn't run far before it disappears into the sand. This makes it easier to rock hop down the gully. Before you know it, you're on the flat again, not far from the track leading up to the mine.

You tighten the shoulder straps on your backpack and then look at Paulie. "We need to get to camp as quickly as possible. Keep low. Use the scrub for cover. It's about two miles, I reckon."

Paulie swallows and cinches up his straps.

"Oh and listen out for rattlers!"

"Great," Paulie says. "If the smugglers don't get us the snakes will."

"You'll be fine, Paulie. Just follow me."

You take off in a half trot, dodging from bush to bush. You figure you've gone about half way to camp, when you hear the growl of a diesel motor in the distance. But how?

When you look through the scrub, the truck is coming across the flatland, leaning awkwardly to the left. The truck is making good speed, despite what you've done to it.

"Oh no!" Paulie cries.

You stop behind a big clump of saltbush. "Keep low, I don't think they've seen us yet."

From the direction the men are driving, it looks as though

they are sticking to the track you saw from up the hill. Thankfully, this track goes to the main road, not directly to the camp. Once on the road however, there will be nothing stopping them from driving a mile or so down to the campground turnoff. As if to confirm your theory, the truck turns slightly away from you as the dirt road arcs around to avoid a dry wash.

"Come on," you say. "We've still got time." You slip off your pack and let it drop to the ground. "We can come back for these later. Right now, we need to run!"

Like a pair of jackrabbits, you and Paulie jink back and forth between clumps of saltbush as you head towards camp.

Off to your left, the truck's flattened tires kick up a cloud of dust. Luckily, the wind is blowing the cloud in your direction giving you some extra cover.

The truck has just reached the main road when you and Paulie skid exhausted into camp.

"Mister Jackson!" you pant, out of breath. "Smug–smugglers!"

Mister Jackson looks up. "What are you on about?"

"Fossil smugglers," you say. "Paulie and I caught them up at the old mine. They tried to bury us!"

Paulie points towards the road. "They're coming in that truck! And they have a pistol."

"What happened to their truck?" Mister Jackson says when he sees the funny lean on the truck.

"I stabbed their tires to slow them down," you say.

"Maybe that wasn't such a good idea."

Mister Jackson gives you a hard look. "Because now they have to come to camp for more transport. What were you thinking!"

You look down at your feet. "We just…"

Mister Jackson shakes his head and then turns to the other students milling about. "Okay everyone listen up. I want everyone on the bus right now! Duck down below the windows and stay there until I say otherwise."

As you wait in line to climb aboard, Mister Jackson runs to a locker on the side of the bus and pull out a flare gun. From a small box he takes out a cartridge and slots it into the chamber before closing the gun up and slipping it into the back of his shorts, under his t-shirt.

Paulie's pushing you in the back, so you run up the step and duck down beside the driver's seat. The students, sitting on the floor further down the bus, chatter nervously.

"Shush everyone," you say.

The gravel crunches as the smuggler's truck roars into camp and skids to a stop about twenty yards from the bus.

"Quiet everyone! I want to hear what's going on."

A hush falls over the bus. You take a quick peek outside.

"Looks like you've had problems with your truck," Mister Jackson says as he approaches the men.

The men have thrown a tarp over the bones in the back of the truck. Neither of them look happy. They face Mister Jackson while the other parents stand back, unsure of what to do.

The men are covered in dust.

"Someone in your group has stabbed our tires. So we'll need to borrow your bus."

"I'm afraid that isn't an option," Mister Jackson says. Your teacher reaches into his pocket and pulls out his cell phone. However, I'll call for someone to come and tow you to town."

"You seem to have misunderstood me," the bigger of the two men says. "I wasn't really asking." The man pulls out his pistol and points it at Mister Jackson. "Now give me the keys and get those brats off the bus."

Mister Jackson raises his hands, palms out. "Whoaa… Steady there. We're not looking for any trouble here."

The man scowls. "Well then, do as I say!" He waves the gun towards the bus. "Now!"

"Okay, okay, take it easy." Mister Jackson walks to the bus and pokes his head through the door. "Everyone off the bus. Go sit on the picnic tables by the fire. Don't worry – everything's going to be fine."

The students do as they're told. A couple have been crying. You're about to join them outside when you hear rattling under the bus. You freeze. Then you hear the distinctive sound of the snake again. It seems to be moving towards the front steps.

You have an idea. Rather than getting off the bus, you duck back down.

You listen as Mister Jackson gives the man the keys.

"Now get out of my way," man says.

There is a scrunch of gravel as the men make their way to the bus. When you think they are about to climb aboard, you stand up and start down the steps, stopping at the bottom one.

You and the man are eye to eye.

"I said, get off!" he yells.

You wipe his spittle off your face with the back of your hand. You're about to climb down when the rattlesnake strikes.

"Yeow!" the man yells, throwing himself back.

But the snake is on the attack. It whips its head forward and strikes him again.

When the man grabs at his leg and falls to the ground, the pistol skids on the dirt. The second man moves to pick it up.

"I wouldn't do that if I were you," Mister Jackson says, leveling the flare gun at the man's face. "Now back up! Put your hands on your head!"

The snake backs off at the sound of Mister Jackson shouting and slithers off into the sagebrush. The second man does as he's told.

You leap off the bus, pick up the pistol, and run behind Mister Jackson.

The man on the ground has his cuff pulled up and is staring at the puncture wounds in his calf. His face is twisted in pain and the area around the wounds is already red and swollen. "I need a hospital," he moans.

Mister Jackson takes the pistol from your shaking hand and sends you to sit with the other students.

"Tie them up," Mister Jackson says to the other parents. "I'll phone the police."

Once the men have been secured, and police phoned, Mister Jackson grabs a snakebite kit from the first aid box and moves towards the injured man. "Just take it easy, you'll live."

Paulie sidles up next to you. "Did you know the snake was there?" he asks.

You tell him about hearing the rattle just before you got off the bus and how you planned to get the man to stop by the steps in the hope that the rattler would strike.

"Who needs a gun when you have a prairie rattler to do your dirty work, eh?" Paulie says.

"Snakes are our friends," you say, quoting Paulie's words back to him. "Isn't it their job to clean up the vermin?"

"Yeah, I suppose it is." He gives you a huge grin. "Did you know that some vermin, especially rats, have teeth that can grow five inches in a single year? They wear them down by gnawing on things. And some carry plague … and… and…"

Paulie keeps waffling on about rats, but you're not really listening. Instead, you're thinking about the adventure you've had.

When you see the flashing lights of the police car and ambulance in the distance, you know that this time you've been lucky. What would have happened if you'd chosen differently?

Congratulations, this part of your story may be over, but now you can try another path and see what happens when you make different choices. It is time to make a decision. Do you:

Go back to the start and read a different track? **P1**

Or

Go to the list of choices and start reading from another part of the story? **P136**

You have decided to rush back to camp.

You and Paulie slide back down the rock and skirt the pool towards the watercourse.

"Watch your step, Paulie, these rocks are a bit slippery. The last thing we need is an injury."

But slippery rocks are only a problem for a short distance. Before long, most of the water has seeped into the sand and disappeared.

"The stream's gone underground again," Paulie says. "It must only run on the surface when it's raining."

"Which, by the look of the sky behind us, could be any moment."

Paulie looks back over his shoulder at the dark grey clouds billowing up like menacing waves. "Where did those come from?"

"I don't know, but if it rains higher up the hill there could be a flash flood. We'd better get out of the streambed just in case."

A bolt of lightning flashes towards the ground. Seconds later, a huge BOOM echoes across the sky.

"Whoaaa!" Paulie says. "That was a beauty."

Another bolt streaks towards the ground. FLASH! BOOM!

"Come on, Paulie. Let's keep moving. Those smugglers will probably head back to the truck before this storm hits."

You and Paulie move out of the streambed and pick up the pace. But the storm is gaining on you.

Fifteen minutes later, just as you hit the flat land of the prairie, the storm front hits. The wind gusts, and hailstones the size of walnuts, pelt down.

"Ouch!" Paulie yells. "That hurts!"

"Quick, over here, under this sagebrush. Hold your pack over your head," you say.

Rushing over to the nearest patch of scrub, you and Paulie cower under its thin branches, your packs held up as shields. The lumps of ice beating on your packs sound like some crazy drummer. Strong gusts fling fine particles of sand like miniature missiles, stinging your exposed skin.

"Holy moly," Paulie says, picking up a huge hailstone. "This is awesome!"

You're not sure 'awesome' is the word you'd use. But you have to admit that Paulie has a point. The storm has moved in so fast, and its power is so strong, it's taken you by surprise. The sky has gone so dark, it's like the sun has set.

Between two flashes of lightning, you see the smugglers running for their truck, their hands and arms held over their heads to protect them from the hail.

Unfortunately, straggly sagebrush isn't the greatest hiding place. And, you're directly in the smugglers' path.

"Down," you whisper. "Lay flat, maybe they won't see us."

It was a poor plan, one doomed to failure.

"Hey, Walter. Look! It's those two brats!"

"Well I'll be…" the other man says.

"What do we do?" Paulie squeaks.

"Leave the packs and run for it!"

Paulie takes off behind you. You've only got a hundred yards head start on the smugglers, but that's better than nothing. Unfortunately, because of the men in your path, the only way you can go is away from camp. You'll have to go in a big arc, if you're to make it back without the men getting hold of you.

The storm strengthens. Hailstones pound the ground, kicking up little craters in the sand. Lightning strikes the ground a quarter of a mile to your right. The men are gaining on you.

Paulie gasps. "I can't run any further. Can't breathe in this dust." He slows down.

It's then that you see the dark grey funnel dropping from the bottom of one of the clouds towards the ground.

Paulie looks up, his eyes wide. "Holy moly. A tornado!"

The men are only 60 yards away when the funnel picks them up and swirls them into the air. You're not sure if the high-pitched screams you hear are the men, or the wind. But you don't have time to think about that now, the funnel is still coming right at you. Grabbing Paulie's arm, you throw yourself onto the ground and cover your head with your arms.

Dust swirls. The wind whips at your clothes. The edge of the funnel misses you by twenty feet, scattering sand and pebbles in its wake. The tornado then races on across the prairie.

"Phew," you say. "That was close!"

"You're telling me," he says.

"Those poor men."

"Yeah, even criminals don't deserve that. Still there have been cases of people being dropped safely some miles away after being picked up by a tornado."

"Really?" you ask.

Paulie nods. "There was this kid in Alabama who got sucked up out of his bunk bed and was dropped alive. He had a few cuts and bruises, but lived to tell the tale."

"Well let's hope those men get dropped into prison, that's where they belong."

You brush the dust and sand off your clothes, and watch as the dark mass of clouds move further off to the north, its funnel touching the ground occasionally along the way.

"I hope the camp is okay," you say. "We'd better get going and find out."

You're about to walk off when you see a couple of strange looking lumps lying on the ground about 50 yards off to the north. "What're those?"

Paulie peers at the strange formations. "Let's go find out."

At first they look like rocks protruding out of the sand. But as you near, you see it is the two men. They look unconscious.

"Quick, let's tie them up before they wake up." you say.

"Tie them up with what?" Paulie asks.

You think a moment. Then notice the men's sturdy boots. "Use their bootlaces."

Kneeling down, you tie the man's wrists behind his back, watching for any sign that he's waking up. Paulie does the same with the other man. Once they're secure, you'll breathe easier.

"Right, that should do it," you say standing up. "They're not going anywhere."

"Now what?" Paulie asks, admiring his handiwork.

You look towards the camp. It's still at least a mile away. "We can't leave them here alone. They'll run away."

When you look back towards Paulie, he has a big grin on his face. "Not without shoes they won't."

"Now you're talking!"

You get the men's boots off, just as they begin to move.

"Good work, Paulie. Now, let's go get help."

Carrying the men's boots, the two of you jog towards camp.

"I just thought of something," you say. "It's not that far to their truck, what if they get loose and drive off?"

Paulie reaches into his pocket and pulls out of set of keys. "I took these while I was tying the guy up."

"Stole them, you mean?"

"I've borrowed them," Paulie says. "He can have them back once the police arrive."

And with that sorted, you head straight back to camp.

Congratulations, you've finished this part of your story. But there are more tracks you can read and more adventures to have. Maybe things won't end up so well next time if you make different choices.

It is time to make a decision. Do you:

Go back to the start and try a different path? P1

Or

Go to the list of choices and start reading another chapter? P136

(The list of choices is also a good place to double-check to make sure you haven't missed parts of the story.)

Animal Facts

Rattlesnake facts:

Although there are many different types of rattlesnakes, the only rattlesnake that lives in Montana, where this story is set, is the prairie rattlesnake. Prairie rattlesnakes have a triangular head, narrow neck and a thickset body. Rattlesnakes swallow their prey whole.

The largest rattlesnake in the U.S. is the Eastern Diamondback which can grow to over 8 feet in length. Prairie rattlesnakes are smaller and only grow up to 5 feet or so. Their color varies, from light green to a blotchy brown.

Prairie rattlesnakes have heat sensors between their nostrils and eyes. Hollow fangs inject poison into their prey. More poison is injected in hunting bites than when striking defensively. (Why waste good poison?) At the end of a rattlesnake's tail is a rattle that warns predators of the snake's presence.

More than 8,000 people are bitten by venomous snakes in the US each year, but the average number of deaths from snakebite is under a dozen.

Rattlesnakes belong to a group of snakes called pit vipers. They have good vision both night and day.

Prairie Dog facts:

Prairie dogs can grow as long as three feet from head to tail and weigh from 1.5 to 3.3 pounds.

Sometimes they are mistaken for squirrels, but can be

identified by their thicker body and shorter tail. Prairie dogs are herbivores and get their water from the plants they eat.

The animals live in burrows in flat open grassland. Colonies can cover quite a large area (twenty-five acres or more). Burrows can be as deep as 14 feet underground and run for 30 yards or more. A family group usually comprises a male and three or four females. Females give birth to 4 or more pups depending on conditions. After being born, pups stay underground for up to 8 weeks before appearing above ground in mid-May to early June.

The main predators for prairie dogs are ferrets, snakes, coyotes, badgers, and birds of prey.

Pronghorn facts:

Pronghorn antelope live in open sagebrush country and grasslands. They migrate south during harsh winters. Females breed in September and males shed their horns in November. Sometimes males will fight to the death for control of females.

Pronghorns are the fastest land animals in North America and can reach speeds of 55 miles per hour (but only over a short distance). They stand just over four feet tall and weigh approximately 140 pounds for males, and 105 pounds for females.

Bison facts:

Bison stand up to six and a half feet tall and can weigh over a ton. They are grazers, eating grass, herbs and shrubs. Like cows, they regurgitate their food and chew the cud before the food is fully digested.

Females are called cows, while males are known as bulls.

Bison once covered the Great Plains and were an important source of food, and raw materials for the Plains Indians. It is estimated that settlers killed over 50 million of these animals.

Bison are speedy and can run at up to 45 miles per hour.

Dinosaur Facts

Tyrannosaurus Rex facts:

T. Rex was a massive animal – nearly 40 feet long, over 13 feet tall and weighing six tons or more. They lived 68 - 66 million years ago in the upper Cretaceous Period. T. Rex were one of the biggest ever land-based carnivores. They had massive heads and teeth the size of bananas. T. Rex's huge heads were balanced by their big strong tails, and although their front arms were short, they were very powerful.

So far scientists have identified over 50 different Tyrannosaurus species. Some scientists believe that these animals had feathers on parts of their bodies.

Ankylosaurus facts:

Imagine a cross between a tank and a 30 foot lizard! Ankylosaurus were nearly 6 feet tall and 20 to 30 feet long with tough bone armor on their back and a wicked looking club-shaped tails which they swung around in defense.

For added protection, rows of spikes ran down their body and horns grew from their heads.

The only weakness was the animal's soft underbelly.

Because they weighed in at 3 to 4 tons, attacking an Ankylosaurus was no easy task, even for a T. Rex.

Ankylosaurus was a herbivore and ate large quantities of plant material each day.

It lived 68 to 66 million years ago.

Troodon facts:

Troodons lived in the Cretaceous period, approximately 77 million years ago. They were small by dinosaur standards, growing about three feet tall and eight feet from their nose to the tips of their tails.

Troodons were slender with long hind limbs. This suggests they were able to run quite fast. They also had curved claws on their second toe (not so good for climbing sandstone arches).

Because of their large eyes, scientists think that Troodons may have been nocturnal. They are thought to be one of the most intelligent of the dinosaurs, with a large brain compared to their body size. Like many dinosaurs, Troodons laid eggs.

Tylosaurus facts:

Nothing was safe when a Tylosaurus was about. Tylosaurus (a type of mosasaurs) were the dominant predator of the western inland seaway in the late cretaceous period (85 - 80 million years ago). This seaway split what is now North America, from the Gulf of Mexico to Canada.

Tylosaurus reached lengths of 45 feet and weighed 7 tons or more. Tylosaurus had a long alligator-like snout, front and back flippers, and a broad powerful tail used for rapid acceleration.

Scientists believe that Tylosaurus used its snout as a battering ram. Once stunned, the Tylosaurus would clamp on to its prey with its powerful jaws and large cone-shaped teeth to keep the stunned prey from escaping. Once the Tylosaurus' prey was disabled, it would be swallowed whole.

The main diet for Tylosaurus was fish, sharks, plesiosaurs and other smaller mosasaurs.

Although not a true dinosaur Tylosaurus lived and became extinct at the same time. It is thought to be a relative of the monitor lizard. Dinosaurs and lizards (which are reptiles) are different. Many scientist believe dinosaurs were warm blooded (reptiles are cold blooded). Also their posture, skeleton, teeth etc are different. It is believed that many dinosaurs had feathers and were relatives to modern birds. Remember, turtles and snakes are reptiles yet quite different to a T. Rex.

Daspletosaurus facts:

Related to the T. Rex, Daspletosaurus lived 77 - 74 million years ago.

Although slightly smaller than the T. Rex, Daspletosaurus was an aggressive and formidable predator at the top of the food chain.

It walked on two hind legs and had small, yet powerful, front arms. Its skull alone could reach 39 inches in length. Nose to tail, Daspletosaurus 25 - 30 feet in length weren't uncommon.

Daspletosaurus had teeth! Lots of teeth.

It is thought that Daspletosaurus lived in social groups, possibly hunting as a pack. Yikes!

Velociraptor facts:

Well known for their role in the movie *Jurassic Park*, Velociraptor, which lived 75 - 75 million years ago, were actually smaller than portrayed in the movie. In reality they were about the size of a turkey, with sickle-shaped claws on its feet and feathers over most of its body. They had wing-like arms, but couldn't fly (although some scientists believe they could climb trees using the sharp talons on their feet).

Full grown, Velociraptors could reach 6 feet in length and weigh over 30 pounds.

Velociraptors hunted and scavenged for food. They were fast on their feet, and capable of bringing down prey up to 50% larger than themselves.

Scientists believe modern birds evolved from dinosaurs similar to the Velociraptor.

Pachycephalosaurs facts

Estimated to be about 15 feet long and over 900 pounds, Pachycephalosaurs went extinct with the last of the dinosaurs about 65 million years ago. Pachycephalosaurs' most distinguishing features were the thick plate of bone on their head. Bony knobs surrounded this plate, with blunt horns protruding from the back of it. More boney bumps covered their snouts making them quite strange looking.

Scientists believe its diet was most probably leaves, seeds, insects and fruit, rather than tougher, more fibrous plants due to their small, serrated teeth.

Pterodactyl facts:

Not officially dinosaurs, Pterodactyls were flying reptiles that lived from the Jurassic period some 150 - 148 million years ago, to the time of their extinction by the late Cretaceous period 65 million years ago. They were the first vertebrates (animals with a backbone) known to have developed powered flight.

Their wings were made from skin and muscle stretched between their front fingers and hind legs and had a span from 3 to 35 feet, depending on species.

These animals had long thin heads with a crest made of soft tissue. Their mouths contained 90-or more cone-shaped teeth that got smaller as they went back into the animal's head.

With sharp eyesight and even sharper talons, they preyed on fish and other small animals.

Some of the larger species could have flown long distances.

Einiosaurus facts:

A dinosaur similar in appearance to Triceratops. Its name means 'buffalo lizard'. They grew to approx 20 feet in length and over 6 feet high.

Like the modern day rhino, Einiosaurus had a horn in the middle of its face, but Einiosaurus' horns slope forward and down like an old-fashion can opener.

Einiosaurus had teeth capable of eating the toughest plants, but they were also thought to have died in vast numbers during times of drought.

They lived in the late Cretaceous, approx 74 million years ago in the Montana region.

Triceratops facts:

Triceratops lived approximately 68 million years ago. That's 68,000,000 if you write it out in full.

With its bony frill (like a large collar) and three big horns (tri means three), Triceratops is estimated to have weighed from 13,000 to 26,000 pounds. One skull recovered was over 8 feet long, nearly a third of the animal's body length.

Because of unusual formations on the animal's skin, some scientists think Triceratops might have been covered in bristles, or similar.

One of the largest land animals ever, Triceratops was a herbivore that grazed on shrubs, and possibly, like modern day elephants, knocked over larger trees to feed.

Triceratops had a mouth full of teeth. Rows and rows of them, suggesting they were able to eat the toughest of plants.

Damage to skulls found show that triceratops used its head as a battering ram, possibly in combat with predators.

More 'You Say Which Way' books.

Pirate Island
Dragons Realm
Volcano of Fire
The Creepy House
Between The Stars
Lost in Lion Country
Once Upon An Island
In the Magician's House
Secrets of Glass Mountain
Danger on Dolphin Island
The Sorcerer's Maze Jungle Trek
The Sorcerer's Maze Adventure Quiz

YouSayWhichWay.com

List of Choices

Please leave a review of this book on Amazon
Reviews help others know if this book is right for them. It only takes a moment. Thanks from the You Say Which Way team.

138

Preview: The Creepy House

Shhh! What's that noise?

Your family got a cheap deal on a bigger house, and the day you move in you find out why. Right next door is a creepy old place that looks like the set for a horror movie. Your family says it has character but you think it might have rats … or worse.

Your cat is locked in the spare room while the movers are going in and out so she doesn't get lost. The cat was a bribe from your family to accept moving away from all your friends. She's small and gray and came from the animal shelter. You've thought of the perfect name for her: Ghost.

After the movers have gone and the doors are shut downstairs, you let Ghost out to explore her new home. She comes into your room as you're putting away the last of your books and jumps on your bed.

"Hello Ghost. Do you like your new home?"

You settle down next to her with your book. It's called *Between the Stars* and it's about a weird spaceship of sleeping travelers who wake up for adventures. It's really good but you're distracted by a tapping at the window. That's odd, it's a second story window.

There's a tall tree just outside, it must be making the noise. You open the window and see that a branch is caught on some old wires. You untangle the wires just as you hear "Dinner's ready!" from downstairs. Your stomach growls, you don't need telling twice.

When you come back, Ghost isn't on your bed anymore and you can feel a breeze from the open window. As you start to shut it, you see your cat disappearing inside a window next door. She has climbed through the tree over to that spooky house.

"Ghost! Ghost! Puss, puss, puss!"

Through tattered drapes you can make out an old fashioned bed over there. A movement in the opposite room catches your eye and then you recognize yourself reflected in a long grimy mirror. You shiver. There's no sign of Ghost.

It is time to make your first decision. Do you:

Go over to the house and try to get your cat back?

Or

Leave the window open and wait for her to return?

Preview: The Sorcerer's Maze - Jungle Trek

One moment you were at home reading a book and now you're standing in the jungle, deep in the Amazon rainforest.

Beside you flows a slow-moving river, murky brown from all the silt it carries downstream. Monkeys screech in the tall trees across the water. The air is hot and buzzing with insects. As you watch, the tiny flying creatures gather together in an unnatural cloud formation and then separate to form words:

WELCOME they spell in giant letters.

This is crazy you think.

NOPE, IT'S NOT CRAZY spell the insects. THIS IS THE START OF THE SORCERER'S MAZE.

The insect cloud bursts apart and the tiny creatures buzz off. What's next, you wonder?

Twenty yards away two kids, about your age, stand beside a boat with a small outboard motor attached to its stern. The boat has a blue roof to protect its occupants from the hot tropical sun.

They both smile and wave.

The girl walks towards you. "Do you want a ride upriver?" she asks. "My brother and I know the Amazon well."

"Do you work for the sorcerer?" you ask. "He designed the maze, didn't he?"

The girl nods. "Yes. My brother and I are his apprentices. The sorcerer wants you to have company while you're here."

The two of you walk back down to the river's edge.

"This is Rodrigo. I'm Maria."

You drop your daypack into the dugout and hold out your hand. "Hi Rodrigo, interesting looking boat."

Rodrigo shakes your hand. "It does the job. But before we can go upriver," he says, pulling a piece of paper out of his pocket, "the sorcerer wants me to ask you a question. If you get it right, we can leave."

"And if not?" you ask.

"I've got more questions," the boy says, patting his

pocket. "I'm sure you'll get one right eventually." He unfolds the paper. "Okay, here's your first question. Which of the following statements is true?"

It is time to make a decision. Which do you choose?
The Amazon River has over 3000 known species of fish.
Or
The Amazon River has less that 1000 known species of fish.

Preview: In the Magician's House

You can't remember a time when you didn't live and work in the Magician's house. It is cloaked in mystery and you explore it every day.

There are many rooms, but you have to catch them while you can.

You find the kitchen easily most mornings. You just follow the lovely smells and don't think too hard about it. Perhaps your recent dreams help you get to breakfast without much trouble. More likely, it's because the Magician wants his breakfast – why would he hide a place he wants you to go to?

You can find a lot of places in the house, especially the rooms you know about. You also have a knack for finding rooms you've never been to before, and for this reason, you're often asked to fetch things by the others who work in the house. They seem to get lost far more often than you do. Sometimes you find other servants in the corners of rooms and give them a friendly pat to bring them out of a 'drawing room dream'. That is what the cook, Mrs Noogles, calls them. Dreams swirl around in the Magician's house just like dust does in the corners of other houses. Little stories get. stuck in the crannies. Just for a moment, while you're sweeping a corner, you can find yourself running across a green field, speaking to a great crowd, steering an iron horse through twisty roads, or picking ripe strawberries in a bright warm field. Those are the dreams and they are quickly over, but other times you're transported to different places. So you watch where you step.

It is very early in the morning, and you wake up in your turret. It is your own tower with a winding staircase down to the house.

Something cold nestles against your cheek. You put your hand out. It's that frog again.

The red frog stares at you. Lifting it from the pillow, you place it next to a water-filled glass bowl on a shelf. The rest of the shelf contains treasures and oddities that you've picked up, and some, like the frog, that seem to have followed you home. The frog sits perfectly still and turns to stone, but you know it is likely to change back and follow you like a naughty puppy. No matter – it's harmless and has never gotten you into trouble. Although you hope you don't tread on it by accident one day when it isn't a stone.

The sky is dark purple, with one last star valiantly blinking as the rising sun starts to turn your corner of the world into day. You love looking out of your tower window and catching the day starting like this – in this moment the whole world is magic, not just the place you live.

Down the spiral staircase, on the next floor, you wash the sleep from your eyes and put on fresh clothes. A sound like a marble falling down the stairs becomes the sound of a rubber ball until the red frog appears with a final splat. He takes a quick dip in the big jug of water you keep for him there. When he jumps out, he doesn't leave any wet marks on the flagstone floor. He seems to absorb moisture. The jug is now only half full so you top it up.

By the window, a row of ants march across the floor. The frog jumps over to the row of insects, and whips out his tongue to catch ant after ant until the column is gone. If only getting your breakfast was that easy.

Through the window are the buildings of London – St Paul's cathedral is a beautiful dome by the river Thames. Horses and carts make deliveries down the twisty lanes. Much of London is still sleeping, but servants are stirring to light the fires and make their master's breakfast. You must tend to your master too.

As you move further down the turret, you wonder which room it will join with today. Sometimes it will deliver you to a hallway which easily gets you to the servant's staircase and down to the kitchen, but often there is another destination at the foot of the stairs. Things are seldom as they appear. You have learned to be cautious in case you step in a lily pond in the wide conservatory or walk into the shiny suit of armor which appears in different places each day.

The stairs wind down until you meet up with the rest of the house. Here is where you're usually faced with your first choice for the day. This morning, a wide corridor with arched ceilings, stretches off to the left and right. Embroidered tapestries hang along oak paneled walls.

To your left, the corridor ends abruptly. A suit of armor stands at the dead end, its bright metallic form is leaning slightly forward, its gloved hand is holding up the edge of the last tapestry. Behind the tapestry is the corner of what looks like a small door.

In the corridor to your right is an impassable hole in the floor with a ladder poking out. The carpet is ripped and torn around the hole as though a bomb has gone off in the night. That's weird. You didn't hear an explosion.

You've never seen this hole or the secret door behind the tapestry before.

It's time to make your first decision for the day. Do you:
Go down the ladder into the hole?
Or
Take the secret door behind the suit of armor?

Preview: Secrets of Glass Mountain

With the screech of diamonds on smooth black rock, a troop of Highland Sliders comes skidding to a stop ten yards from you and your schoolmates.

"That's what I want to do when I leave school," says Dagma. "Being a Highland Slider looks like so much fun."

Another classmate shakes his head. "Yeah, but my cousin went mining and struck it rich on his first trip out. Now he owns two hydro farms and his family live in luxury."

You look around the small settlement where you grew up. It's a beautiful place, high on the Black Slopes of Petron. Far below, past the sharp ridges and towering pinnacles, the multicolored fields of the Lowlands stretch off into the distance. At the horizon, a pink moon sits above a shimmering turquoise sea.

But the beauty isn't enough to keep you here. You could never be a farmer or a merchant. You've always dreamed of travel and adventure.

Maybe mining is the right thing to do. You imagine heading off into the wild interior looking for diamonds and the many secrets these glass mountains contain. Imagine striking it rich!

Or do you become a slider like so many others from your family? What would happen to your home without the protection of the Highland Sliders? How would people move around the dangerous slopes, from settlement to settlement, without their expert guidance? And who would stop the Lowlanders from invading?

Your part in this story is about to begin. You will leave school at the end of the week and it's time for you to choose your future.

It is time to make your first decision. Do you:
Start cadet training to become a slider?
Or
Go to mining school so you can prospect for diamonds?

Preview: Pirate Island

Your family is on holiday at a lush tropical island resort in the Caribbean. But you're not in the mood to sit around the pool with the others, you want to go exploring. Rumors say that pirate treasure has been found in these parts and you're keen to find some too. With a few supplies in your daypack, you fill your drinking bottle with water, grab your mask and snorkel, and head towards the beach.

You like swimming, but you've been planning this treasure hunt for months and now is as good a time as any to start. The beach outside the resort stretches off in both directions. To your right, it runs past the local village, where children laugh as they splash and play in the water. Palm trees line the shore and brightly-colored fishing boats rest on the sand above the high tide mark. Past the village, way off in the distance, is a lighthouse.

To your left, the sandy beach narrows quickly and soon becomes a series of rocky outcrops jutting into the sea. Steep cliffs rise up from the shore to meet the stone walls of an old and crumbling fortress.

You have four hours before your family expects you back.

It is time to make your first decision. Do you:
Go right and head towards the lighthouse?
Or:
Go left and head towards the rocks and the old fortress?

Preview: Between the Stars.

In a sleep tank on the space ship *Victoria*, your dreaming cap teaches you as you float.

You first put on a dreaming cap for the space sleep test. Although you thought it looked like you had an octopus on your head, you didn't joke about it. Nobody did. Everyone wanted to pass the test and go to the stars. Passing meant a chance to get out of overcrowded Londinium. If you didn't pass you'd likely be sent to a prison factory in Northern Europa. Nobody wanted to go there. Even though Britannica hasn't been a good place lately, Europa was said to be worse.

When the judge sentenced you to transportation for stealing that food, you sighed inside with relief. You knew transportation was the chance of a better life on a faraway planet, but only if you passed the sleep test.

You lined up with other hopefuls and waded into a pool of warm sleep jelly. They were all young, like you, and they all looked determined.

"Stay calm," the robot instructed. "Breathe in slowly through your mouthpiece and relax."

Nearby, a young woman struggled from the pool. She pulled out her breathing plug and gasped for breath.

"Take her back," said a guard. You knew what that meant – back to prison and then the factories. A convict sneered at the poor girl, the cruel look on his face magnified by a scar running down one cheek.

In your short time in prison, you had learned there were people who would have been criminals no matter what life they'd been born to. Something told you that he was one of them.

You put him out of your mind and concentrated on doing what the robot said. You thought of the warm porridge you'd had every morning in the orphanage growing up. The sleeping jelly didn't seem so strange then. When your head was submerged you breathed in slowly.

As the jelly filled your lungs you fought against thoughts of drowning. You'd listened at the demonstration and knew it was oxygenated. *This must be what it's like to be a fish*, you thought as you moved forward through the thick fluid, *I only have to walk through to the other side.*

Closing your eyes, you moved forward through the thick warm jelly. "Relax," you told yourself. "You can do this."

You opened your eyes just in time to see the scar-faced youth about to knock your breather off. Thankfully the jelly slowed his punch and you ducked out of the way just in time. Then a moment later, you were on the other side being handed a towel.

"This one's a yes," intoned a man in a white coat. He slapped a bracelet on your wrist and sent you down a corridor away from your old life. As you exited, you just had time to hear the fate of the scar-faced youth. "He'll do. Take him to the special room."

Days of training followed. You often joined other groups of third class passengers but you didn't see Scar-Face among them. You passed all the tests and then one day, you got into a sleep tank beside hundreds of others. Your dreaming cap would teach you everything you'd need to know in your new life.

You were asleep when the *Victoria* was launched into space. You slept as the *Victoria* lost sight of the Earth and then its star, the sun.

And here you are, years later, floating in sleep fluid and learning with your dreaming cap. Or you were. Because now you hear music. Oxygen hisses into your sleeping chamber and the fluid you have been sleeping in starts to drain away. Next time you surface, you'll breathe real air, something that your lungs haven't done in a long time.

"Sleeper one two seven six do you accept this mission? Sleeper, please engage if you wish to awaken for this mission. Sleeper, there are other suitable travelers for this mission. Do you choose to wake?"

Passengers can sleep the entire journey if they want. They can arrive at the new planet without getting any older. First class passengers will own land and riches when they arrive but you're third class, you have nothing. Groggily, you listen to the voice. If you choose to take on a mission you can earn credit for the new planet – even freedom – but you could also arrive on the new planet too old to ever use your freedom.

"Sleeper, do you accept the mission?"

It is time to make your first decision.

Do you want to wake up and undertake this mission?

Or

Do you wait for a different mission or wait to land on the new planet?

Preview: Lost in Lion Country

You only jumped out of the Land Rover for a second to take a photo. How did the rest of your tour group not notice? You were standing right beside the vehicle taking photos of a giraffe. It's not like you walked off somewhere.

The next thing you know, dust is flying and you're breathing exhaust fumes as the Land Rover races off after the pride of lions your group has been following all morning.

"Wait for me!" you scream as loud as you can. "Wait!"

Unfortunately the sound of the revving diesel engine drowns out your cries. Surely your family will notice you're missing. Maybe that nice teacher lady from Chicago you were chatting to earlier will wonder where you are. Won't the driver realize he's one person short?

You smack yourself on the forehead. This will teach you for sitting alone in the back row while the others on the safari sat up front to hear the driver.

"This is not good," you say to yourself.

What are you going to do now? It's just as well you packed a few emergency supplies in your daypack before you boarded the tour. You have bottled water, a couple of sandwiches, a chocolate bar, your pocket knife and your trusty camera. But these things won't help you if you're seen by hungry lions, leopards, cheetah or one of the other predators that stalks the savannah.

With the vehicle now only a puff of dust in the distance, you notice something else much closer: a pack of hyenas. These scavengers weren't a problem when you were in the vehicle, but now you're on foot and the hyenas are heading your way!

You know from all the books on African wildlife you've read, these dog-like animals can be vicious and have been known to work as a team to bring down much larger animals. They would have no problem making short work of you if they wanted to.

If they find you out here all alone in the Serengeti

National Park, you will be in big trouble.

You look around. What should you do? You know that normally the thing to do when you get lost is to stay put so others can find you when they come looking, but the hyenas make that impossible.

Off to your right is a large acacia tree that you might be able to climb, while on your left is a dried up creek bed.

With the hyenas getting closer you have to move.

You decide to run over and climb up the large acacia tree

The giraffe has moved off to look for more tasty leaves. As you head towards the acacia tree, you keep looking over your shoulder at the pack of hyenas to see if they have spotted you. Luckily, the pack is upwind so their keen noses may have not picked up your scent yet, especially with all the wildebeest and zebra in the area. Still, they are covering the ground faster than you are.

The hyenas are funny looking animals. Unlike dogs, their front legs are slightly longer than their back legs, causing them to slope up towards their head. The members of this pack have light brown bodies with black spots, black faces, and funny rounded ears. If you weren't so afraid of getting eaten by them, you'd stop and take photos.

You're nearly at the tree when one of the hyenas perks up its ears and yips to the others. Suddenly the whole pack is running right at you!

There is no time to waste. You run as fast as you can towards the tree and start looking for a way up. Luckily you can just reach one of the lower branches. You pull yourself up by clamping your legs around the trunk and grabbing every handhold the tree offers. Once you're up on the first limb, the climbing gets easier.

The hyenas are under the tree now, eagerly yipping to each other. A couple of scrawny looking ones take a run at the tree and jump, snapping at your legs. You pull your legs up, and climb a little higher. They circle the tree and stare up at you with their black beady eyes. You are trapped.

You take off your daypack and slip out your camera. No point in missing a great photo opportunity just because you're in a spot of danger. After taking a couple of shots you pull out your water bottle and have a sip. You don't want to drink too much because you're not sure when you'll find more. The grasses on the savannah are turning brown, so you doubt there has been much rain recently. You can see down into the creek from here and it looks bone dry.

Some of the hyenas lie down in the shade of the tree. Their tongues hang out of their mouths. Are they going to wait you out? Do they think you will fall?

You remember reading that hyenas hunt mainly at night. Are they going to hang around in the shade until sundown? How will your family find you if you have to stay up here?

You could be in for a long wait so you try to make yourself comfortable. After wedging your backside in between two branches and hooking your elbow around another, you start to think about what to do to get out of this situation.

It is pretty obvious that climbing down and running for it

would be a really bad idea. The pack of hyenas would have you for lunch before you could get five steps. Maybe when they realize they can't get to you, the pack will move on. Or maybe they will see something that is more likely to provide them with an easy meal.

Just as you're about to lose hope, you see a dust cloud in the distance. It is getting bigger. Is the dust cloud being caused by animals or is it the Land Rover coming back for you?

You stand up and look through the leaves and shimmering haze rising from the grassy plain. Further out on the savannah thousands of wildebeest are on the move.

Surely the cloud is moving too fast to be animals. Then you see the black and white Land Rover owned by the safari tour company. But will they see you? The track is quite some distance away from the tree you are in. You didn't realize you'd come so far.

You scold yourself for not leaving something in the road to mark your position. You yell and wave and wish you'd worn bright clothing so the others could see you through the spindly leaves, but the Land Rover isn't stopping. It drives right past your position and races off in the other direction.

"Come back!" you yell.

You sit down again and think. What can you do? It looks like you're on your own, for now at least.

Then you remember the sandwiches in your daypack. Maybe the hyenas would leave you alone if you gave them some food? But then what happens if they don't leave and you're stuck up the tree for a long time and get hungry?

A pair of vultures land in the bleached branches of a dead tree not far away. Do they know something you don't?

It is time to make a decision. Do you:

Throw the hyenas your sandwiches and hope they will eat them and leave?

Or

Keep your food for later and prepare for a long wait?

Preview: Volcano of Fire

You sit at a long table in the command pod atop one of the twin Pillars of Haramon. The room is filled with the hum of voices. A small robotic bird, unseen by those in the room, hovers in one corner.

The man at the head of the table has three blue-diamond stars pinned to his chest, indicating his rank as chief of the council. Next to him sits a visiting Lowland general, his face as hard as the rock walls of the command pod. Around the table, other important figures from both the Highlands and the Lowlands sit nervously.

Being the newest member of the Highland Council, you have yet to earn your first star, but you have big plans to make your mark.

"Quiet please," the chief says. "We've got important matters to discuss."

The chief's scars are visible, even from your seat at the opposite end of the table. These scars are proof of the many battles and expeditions he has taken part in over his long career and are proof of the dangers of living in the Highlands where the rock under your feet is the slipperiest material imaginable. Black glass.

"Supplies of tyranium crystals have run desperately low," the chief says. "Without tyranium, workers can't move safely around the slopes and that means no progress on the trade routes being built between the Lowlands and the Highlands. If our truce is to last, trade is critical."

As the chief talks, you stare out of the large windows that overlook the slopes below. Further down Long Gully, the second pillar rises from the smooth black slope. A colony of red-beaked pangos squabble with each other for nesting spaces in the cracks near its summit.

To the south are the patchwork fields of the Lowlands, the blue ribbons of the river delta and the turquoise sea. Petron's smallest moon has just risen, pale pink in the morning light, just above the horizon.

"We need to mount an expedition to locate a new source of crystals, and soon," the chief says. "Led by someone we trust."

He turns and looks in your direction. "Someone who knows how to slide on black glass and has the ability to lead a team. Someone with a knowledge of mining and brave enough to take chances when necessary. Are you up for it?" the chief asks, catching you off guard.

"Me?" Sure you've been a troop leader in the Slider Corps and spent some time in mining school, but leading an expedition into new territory? That's quite a responsibility.

The Lowland general stands, rests his hairy knuckles on the table before him, and leans towards your end of the table. "We need someone who is respected by both the Lowlanders and the Highlanders. Someone both sides trust to ensure an equal share of any discoveries."

"That's right," the chief says. "It was you who helped start the peace process. You are the logical choice."

Your part in this story is about to begin. You are being asked to undertake a dangerous mission, one that is important to your community. But are you really qualified? You are young. Surely others would be more suitable. Maybe you should suggest someone more experienced lead the expedition, then you could go back home and live a safe life growing hydro or hunting pangos.

It is time to make your first decision. Do you:
Agree to lead the mission?
Or
Suggest someone else lead the mission?

Preview: Danger on Dolphin Island

It's obvious, from the float plane's window, how Dolphin Island got its name. It is shaped like a dolphin leaping out of the water. A sparkling lagoon forms the curve of the dolphin's belly, two headlands to the east form its tail and to the west another forms the dolphin's nose. As the plane banks around, losing altitude in preparation for its lagoon landing, the island's volcanic cone resembles a dorsal fin on the dolphin's back.

Soon every camera and cell phone is trained on the fiery mountain.

"Wow look at that volcano," shouts a kid in the seat in front of you. "There's steam coming from the crater."

The plane's pontoons kick up rooster-tails of spray as they touch down on the lagoon's clear water. As the plane slows, the pilot revs the engine and motors towards a wooden wharf where a group of smiling locals await your arrival.

"Welcome to Dolphin Island," the resort staff say as they secure the plane, unload your bags, and assist you across the narrow gap to the safety of the small timber wharf.

Coconut palms fringe the lagoon's white-sand beach. Palm-thatched huts poke out of the surrounding jungle. The resort's main building is just beyond the beach opposite the wharf. Between the wharf's rustic planks you can see brightly colored fish dart back and forth amongst the coral. You stop and gaze down at the world beneath your feet.

You hear a soft squeak behind you and step aside as a young man in cut-off shorts trundles past pushing a trolley with luggage on it. He whistles a song as he passes, heading towards the main resort building. You and your family follow.

"Welcome to Dolphin Island Resort," a young woman with a bright smile and a pink flower tucked behind her ear says from behind the counter as you enter the lobby. "Here is the key to your quarters. Enjoy your stay."

Once your family is settled into their beachfront bungalow, you're eager to explore the island. You pack a flashlight, compass, water bottle, pocket knife, matches, mask, snorkel and flippers as well as energy bars and binoculars in your daypack and head out the door.

Once you hit the sand, you sit down and open the guidebook you bought before coming on vacation. Which way should you go first? You're still a little tired from the early morning flight, but you're also keen to get exploring.

As you study the map, you hear a couple of kids coming towards you down the beach.

"Hi, I'm Adam," a blond haired boy says as he draws near.

"And I'm Jane."

The boy and girl are about your age and dressed in swimming shorts and brightly colored t-shirts, red for him and yellow for her. They look like twins. The only difference is that the girl's hair is tied in a long ponytail while the boy's hair is cropped short. Both are brown and have peeling noses. By their suntans you suspect they've been at the resort a few days already.

"What are you reading?" Adam asks.

"It's a guide book. It tells all about the wildlife and the volcano. It also says there might be pirate treasure hidden here somewhere. I'm just trying to figure out where to look first."

Jane clasps her hands in front of her chest and does a tiny hop. "Pirate treasure, really?"

Adam looks more skeptical, his brow creases as he squints down at you. "You sure they just don't say that to get the tourists to come here?"

"No, I've read up on it. They reckon a pirate ship named the *Port-au-Prince* went down around here in the early 1800s. I thought I might go exploring and see what I can find."

"Oh can we help?" Jane asks. "There aren't many kids our age staying at the moment and lying by the pool all day gets a bit boring."

"Yeah," Adam agrees. "I'm sure we could be of some help if you tell us what to do. I've got a video camera on my new phone. I could do some filming."

There is safety in numbers when exploring, and three sets of eyes are better than one. But if you do find treasure, do you want to share it with two other people?

It is time to make your first decision. Do you:

Agree to take Adam and Jane along?

Or

Say no and go hunting for treasure on your own?

Preview: The Sorcerer's Maze

Your feet are sinking into a marshmallow floor. You take a few quick steps and find you can stay on top if you keep moving. How did you get here? One moment you were reading and now you're in a long hallway. The place smells of candy and the pink walls are soft when you poke them.

There is a sign hanging from the ceiling that says: YOU ARE AT THE BEGINNING OF THE SORCERER'S MAZE. But how do you get through to the end of the maze? That is the big question.

Down at the end of the hallway is an old red door. Maybe you should start there? You take a few bouncy steps, your arms held out to help keep your balance. Getting up would be hard. You don't want to fall.

At last you make it to the red door and try the doorknob. It's locked. You pace in a circle to stop from sinking. When you turn back to the door you find another sign. On this sign is a question. Below the question are two possible answers. Maybe answering the question correctly will let you open the door.

The questions reads: What is the largest planet in our solar system?

It's time to make your first decision. You may pick right, you may pick wrong, but still the story will go on. What shall it be?

Jupiter?   Or   Saturn?

162

Preview: Dragons Realm

"Hey, Fart-face!"

Uh oh. The Thompson twins are lounging against a fence as you leave the corner store – Bart, Becks, and Bax. They're actually the Thomson triplets, but they're not so good at counting, so they call themselves twins. Nobody has dared tell them different.

They stare at you. Bart, big as an ox. Becks, smaller but meaner. And Bax, the muscle. As if they need it.

Bart grins like an actor in a toothpaste commercial. "What have you got?" He swaggers towards you.

Becks sneers, stepping out with Bax close behind. "Come on, squirt, hand it over," she calls, her meaty hands bunching into fists.

Your backpack is heavy with goodies. Ten chocolate bars and two cans of tuna fish for five bucks – how could you resist? And now you could lose it all.

The twins form a human wall, blocking the sidewalk. There's no way around them.

Seriously? All this fuss over chocolate? Not again! They've been bullying you and your friends for way too long. There's still time to outsmart them before the bus leaves for the school picnic.

A girl walks between you and the twins. You make your move, sprinting off towards the park next to school. Your backpack is heavy, but you've gained a head start on those numbskulls.

Becks roars.

"Charge," yells Bax,

"Get the snot-head," Bart bellows. Their feet pound behind you as you make it around the corner through the park gate. Now to find a hiding place.

On your right is a thick grove of trees. They'll never find you in there, not without missing the bus to the picnic.

To your left, is a sports field. Behind the bleachers, there's a hole in the fence. If you can make it through that hole, you're safe. They're much too big to follow.

Their pounding footsteps are getting closer. They'll be around the corner soon.

It is time to make a decision. Do you:

Race across the park to the hole in the fence?

Or

Hide from the Thompson twins in the trees?

For more You Say Which Way Adventures visit:

YouSayWhichWay.com